ARMAGEDDON:
Are You Ready?

You'll record 17 dates of events foretold in biblical prophecy

Published by Dauphin Publications
www.daupub.com
E-book available on Kindle

Unless otherwise noted, all Scriptures are taken from the Holy Bible, New American Standard Bible, © 1960, 1962, 1963, 1968, 1971, 1972, 1973, 1977, 1995 by The Lockman Foundation. Used by permission.

ISBN: 9781939438799

Acknowledgments

I owe so much to my family for their patience and support of this long labor of love. They sacrificed many hours, days, vacation days, holidays, and week ends as I dedicated myself to the research and writing of the first book, *Apocalypse Soon*, back in 2003 while we were still living in Puerto Rico. Tita, my dear wife and sweetheart, always knew what was on my heart and let me run with it. Michelle, Michael, and Matthew, my children and gifts from God, also tolerated my apologies for spending the time that ultimately goes to God's glory as others hear about His amazing plan to save them.

And now that this update is ready, 20 years later, again my gratitude goes out to my son, Michael, who has in the interim become a publisher and is now alongside me with this new publication, *ARMAGEDDON: Are You Ready?*

And of course, I am grateful to my Lord Jesus Christ to whom I prayed back in 1980 to give me a passion for where and how to serve Him. He truly endowed me with the hunger and thrill that enabled me to write these books. And there will be more!

Table of Contents

Foreword

*A*pocalypse Soon, the first book published in 2003 was started two weeks after the invasion of Kuwait by Iraq on August 2, 1990. And it was finished at the beginning of another war- the one against terrorism on September 11, 2001. It was born out of war. I guess that's what it took for me to get off my sofa and *do something.* Imagine, it took two wars! But finally, I was moved by the shocking events, the seriousness of my message, the shortness of time, the love of my fellow man, and my Lord Jesus Christ. It was *imperative* then, and urgent now after 20 more years that I get your attention. Right now, everything else that usually fills up our lives, pales in comparison to what I need to share with you.

Just an average person

I believe that if I can make a difference, so can you. If one person, like me, can run shouting the way of escape from impending danger, then so can you. That's my view of the human spirit. And I believe I'm on solid ground.

As a matter of fact, I identify so much with you, that I am strengthened in my resolve to get this message out because I represent the average "joe". Only *this* one is determined to *do something.*

I was born and raised in Chicago, IL with a short three-year period in Ft. Lauderdale. Both my parents worked to make ends meet, thus giving me a lot of responsibility as the oldest of four to help with my brother and two sisters. My father was a welder and carpenter, while my mother drove a school bus, managed a hot dog stand, and delivered telephone books all while being a good mother. Although we were always struggling financially, we kids made it through high school. Having some ambition for college, my brother and I both tried but never finished. Since our finances always needed bolstering, getting a job with the local train engine manufacturer as warehouseman became a priority for me.

Meeting my wife-to-be at a college-sponsored dance was the highlight of my life. Our love for each other has been the fuel for my life for the last 52 years. And it all started in Chicago for the first three years of our marriage as we then moved to Puerto Rico where we made our home for over 30 years until we moved to Orlando in 2006. Three wonderful children, two great grandsons, and the blessings from a few very special friends are the reward for persevering in the face of life's usual challenges.

I've represented major construction and engineering firms as their business development manager over the years and been fortunate to have had the opportunity to also represent Major League's Baseball Chapel in their winter league season in Puerto Rico, serving as a chapel leader and coordinator for twenty-five years.

What has typified my life has been an inner passion to help

people in any way possible. I believe we all must be either giving or receiving as part of the natural cycle of life.

I want to tell you what moved me to write this book and to share its message of hope and salvation as well its wrath and horror. Since September 11, 2001, we've all lost our innocence regarding hatred and the death it brings. Yes, somehow, we all must admit that since the smoke has cleared, we realize we are in a war of good vs. evil; right vs. wrong; truth vs. lies; and yes, even religion vs. religion.

Haven't we all had to ask ourselves, *"Where do I stand? What do I believe? Am I right?"*

These questions moved me to start my search over 32 years ago when the Gulf War broke out. I wanted to know who was telling the truth.

U.S. News & World Report's cover on January 28, 1991, said, **"AMERICA AT WAR"**. Many magazines and newspapers wrote about **"Armageddon"**. The term sounded ominous. But did I know anything about it? No, I didn't. But I wanted to, badly enough to start my own search and to document what I found.

Remember now, an average guy, with no college degree, is suddenly moved to research and study what turns out to be Bible prophecy – a very controversial and difficult subject. But I had the basics: an open mind, the new motivation to start digging, and common sense to check with the experts in the field.

Now, on October 6, 2022, while updating this book, I heard our own president, Joe Biden, proclaimed similar frightening words:

"Nuclear Armageddon" while warning us about Putin's threats. Here we go again!

A ton of reasons

A ton of reasons pulled at my heart to find out what this "Armageddon" was all about. I knew it was a biblical term found in the last book of the Bible, Revelation. But I didn't have the foggiest idea when or how it was prophesied to occur. It is well known that we fear things we don't understand. So, I surely feared, as I'm sure many did, that this "Armageddon," or "end of the world" was just around the corner. If I cared just two cents for my soul, I surely wanted to find out how much time I had to get things right with God. And if I thought like that twenty years ago, how much more while observing the condition of this post-pandemic world. It is time to be sure we are reconciled with our creator.

Since September 11, 2001, when the World Trade Center in New York was destroyed along with part of our Pentagon in Washington, the world was catapulted right up close to the 5-yard line of life and death. Like President Bush once told the nations of the world: "Either you are with us or you're with them…which will it be?" Now we must decide who we will believe regarding the Second Coming, Armageddon, and all this talk of the end times. Will it be *the Bible,* or all the other clamoring voices claiming to know? You will have to ask yourself, "will I hide my head in the sand, or will I check it out for myself? Will I believe traditional explanations of these subjects for tradition's sake? Or will I seek out the secrets held within the pages of the Bible to see why so many are totally convinced of its veracity?"

The prophetic clock is ticking; it's now near midnight. And I want to strongly recommend that you take the weekend off from the beach, the movies, the racetrack, the park, and all the other things that fill up our weekends, to learn what Monday's headlines are all about.

The Challenge

This is about events leading up to Christ's Second Coming and how to prepare yourself. The predictions and instructions come directly from the greatest, most popular and divinely inspired book known to mankind, the **Bible**.

This is not about setting dates for the end. It is not about speculating how all the events will develop. And it is not about religious opinions.

The warnings, the signs, and the evidence are all upon us. Yet the average citizen knows nothing of what's coming next. He may show some curiosity when the tabloid predictors speak out in January about the new year's predictions. He may also show some interest in the mysterious ancient arts, astrology, and the 16th century "prophet", Nostradamus. But how well informed is he on the hundreds of Bible prophecies already fulfilled, and the scores presently falling into place?

Most of the chapters each focus around a specific event prophesied in the Bible. Each event is carefully described from

Scripture, allowing the Word of God to tell the story, with limited comments to provide background and other helpful details. I have purposefully limited my personal opinions because that's not what's important. What's important is what the divine author says.

You will be the one to set the dates, not I. Whether you personally are convinced of the divine inspiration of the Bible or not, you will have the opportunity to record the date of each event in a space provided as these events occur. By keeping a watchful eye, you will be able to prevent yourself from being carried away with the flood of world events. You will be able to let the truth of these prophecies speak for themselves. These events are so close that you are very likely to be around as they unfold. *Let the reliability of God's Word itself convict you* as it is proven in the crucible of time. Then pass this conviction along to your family as time grows shorter.

This book is for the common citizen seeking to find the *real* truth, no matter what sacred cows must fall. It is for the open-minded listener who is willing to step out of the surging mob as they approach the cliff's edge. It is for the sensible, compassionate souls who want to discover the secrets to life, and then help others find their way.

No other time in history has produced such cataclysmic events as the ones we're witnessing. These wrenching experiences move the soul to search for answers. Perhaps many of you are like me. *You really want to know what comes next!*

The words of C.S. Lewis in his <u>Reflections on the Psalms</u> best

X

describe how I view this book, when he says, "This is not a work of scholarship. I am no Hebraist, no higher critic, no ancient historian, no archaeologist. I write for the unlearned about things in which I am unlearned myself. In this book, then, I write as one amateur to another, talking about difficulties I have met, or lights I have gained..."

If one of the greatest Christian authors can humble himself in such a manner, I can do no less. And allow me to give one other word of advice, especially if you ae a newcomer to Bible prophecy. Do not let yourself be discouraged or frustrated when some of the many references and details challenge your memory. There are many dots that require connecting when it comes to finding the timing and order of future events. Go for understanding the main point of each chapter and reread the details later once you are more familiar with the whole subject. Many of the detailed studies and references I quote are from other scholars and from the Bible itself. I felt it was necessary to go into as much detail as I could in order to show those familiar with Bible prophecy, and the skeptic as well, that the proof is in the scripture.

Introduction

History clearly shows us how we have behaved as nations and individuals. And the prophecies written 1900-3000 years ago by biblical authors point the way to the closing chapters of history as we know it.

Yet, despite all of this, the average person doesn't know what is just around the corner as this age reaches its final hour. The hopes and fears of the near future haunt us. Our modern philosophers and soothsayers are the TV journalists, talk show hosts, and politicians. No clear picture is coming from their discourse, rather a confusion and contradiction of what could happen in the hot spots of world attention. At best they guess at what the future lifestyle or economy will be like.

Our individual and collective future is too valuable to leave to such uncertainty. It is too dangerous not knowing what major world events will bring to our lives. And for those who know what these events will be, it is a moral responsibility to shout them from the rooftops of our society.

Prophecies, whether from your local tarot card reader, or from biblical authors, must stand on their own. We can judge them from observing the accuracy of their predictions. And we can judge the sources behind the predictions. Are they *earthly*, coming from man's finite logic; *divine*, coming from God the Creator (100% correct); or *evil*, coming from *demonic sources* deceiving, and pretending to be godly.

Surely one purpose of prophecy, if it is truly divine, is that it brings glory to God and motivates His people to draw closer to Him. When God's creation opens its eyes and pulls down the deceptions created by the modern world, it will be shocked at His greatness. Everything He has said would happen is happening. Hundreds of recorded prophecies have already been fulfilled. There remains an extremely relevant group of prophecies concerning the "last days", "a new world leader", and "the Second Coming of Jesus Christ" yet to be fulfilled.

These remaining unfulfilled prophecies describe our world in the last days. By knowing and understanding what to watch for, you will be spiritually prepared. You will not be deceived or fearful of the events as they develop, because you will not be surprised or caught off guard. This is my purpose for warning the average citizen of these coming events. There is no excuse for God's creation to say they didn't know, when in fact the truths have been written, published, distributed, and studied for thousands of years.

I have identified *seventeen specific events* that will occur in the future. It is very likely they will occur within our generation. After the first two chapters, I've provided a space near the title in each chapter for you to note the date of each event when it occurs. *You set the dates!*

I hope you will be able to distinguish the difference between other "date setting" books and this one. *In this one, you will be setting the dates because of the physical evidence before your own eyes.* Others have boldly erred by "predicting the actual dates" and failing miserably. And that's because they are always in violation of God's statement: "But of that day and hour no one knows, not even the angels of heaven, nor the Son, but the Father alone." (Matthew 24:36)

As a practical tool to help you remember these main events, should you lose or give away this book, I have prepared a summary list as a quick reminder of these events. This summary can be copied and kept in a safe place. And it will help all types of readers, at all levels of faith:

    ° *To the faithful believer,* it will serve as an accurate reminder of events preceding your Lord's return. It will strengthen and assure you. It will help prevent confusion when other voices fill the air. It will help you explain to family and friends how they too can be ready.

    ° *To the doubter,* it will be a bold list of predictions and events to watch for. As the events develop in rapid fire order, the power of God's truth will draw you nearer to Him. This is the real purpose of prophecy. But you must know these prophecies for God's Spirit to be able to convict you of the veracity of His Word, the Bible.

○ *To the hard- hearted,* who is generally unconcerned with the whole issue of moral and godly principles, the summary of events can be a lifesaver. As world events develop, and our lifestyles are threatened, the fact that someone knew about them thousands of years ago, may finally have an impact on them. And the fact you have a summary of these events in your wallet or some other safe place, may one day help save you and your family.

Chapter 1

Signs of the End Times

"...Tell us, when will these things be and what will be the sign of your coming, and of the end of the age?" (Matthew 24:3)

I f you think the present wars and terrorist threats are shocking and threatening to global stability, wait until even more events thunder onto the scene signaling the battle of Armageddon and our Lord's Second Coming. If you are not familiar with these terms, don't worry. The Lord's disciples were not at all acquainted with them either.

Events leading to the "end of the age" will develop over a period of years and will not make a noticeable impression at first. But their gradual increase and effect will create an environment that we will be able to identify, *if we are paying attention.*

Look at the answers Jesus gave to His disciples as they sat one day on the Mount of Olives overlooking Jerusalem:

1) *Famines and Earthquakes Increase*

"...and in various places there will be famines and earthquakes."

(Matthew 24:7)

Of course, we have always had famines and earthquakes. But as communications technology has improved, we are more aware of them happening all over the world. And since populations have increased with time, the effects of these kinds of disasters are increasingly devastating. We also have the unfortunate opportunity to learn about them in our own living rooms as we click through the channels of our TV, seeking to be entertained.

2) *False Cults and Religions Arise*

"And many false prophets will arise and mislead many."

(Matthew 24:11)

"For many will come in My name, saying, 'I am the Christ,' and will mislead many." (Matthew 24:5)

Surely, we have all seen the increase in every sort of New Age religious group popping up everywhere. Leaders of these groups now boldly call themselves the "Son of God", "Messiah", and "prophets from God". They then proceed to lead the spiritually ignorant and young into a maze of truth mixed with lies. The Jonestown mass suicide is the result of this kind of group's teaching. And although we may not hear of more tragedies like Jonestown, millions

2

are being deceived right this moment as they follow teaching that is anti-Christ, totally contrary to Jesus Christ's message of salvation through faith in His sacrifice.

3) *Coldness of Heart and Ungodliness*

"And because lawlessness is increased, most people's love will grow cold."   (Matthew 24:12)

"But realize this, that in the last days difficult times will come. For men will be lovers of self, lovers of money, boastful, arrogant, revilers, disobedient to parents, ungrateful, unholy, unloving, irreconcilable, malicious gossips, without self-control, brutal, haters of good, treacherous, reckless, conceited, lovers of pleasure rather than lovers of God."   (2 Timothy 3:1-4)

What more needs to be said? This describes our generation to the letter. In fact, I'm sure you can name people all around you that fit these descriptions. Is there any wonder why *stress* is a major concern nowadays, when you're forced to experience or fear this kind of behavior from your fellow human?

Before we leave this particular sign, did you notice where this kind of behavior stems from? "Because of lawlessness," this is what happens inside the spirit of man when he goes against the divine guidelines. When *self* and *pleasure* are the focus, the uncontrolled nature of man will

3

lead right straight to where it is now-- front page news reporting brutality and immorality of immense proportions.

4) *Wars and Threats*

"And you will be hearing of wars and rumors of wars...for nation will rise against nation, and kingdom against kingdom..."

(Matthew 24:6, 7)

Very few places on the globe are without conflict. Civil wars, religious wars, tribal wars, rebellions, insurrections, and a myriad of conflicts are all part of the world's landscape today.

A frightening war prompted the writing of this book. On August 2, 1990, Iraq invaded neighboring Kuwait, and the world stood anxiously by to see what would be next. As the United States and the United Nations mobilized their efforts to counter Iraq's plans, I began to examine my understanding of prophecy. Journalists were using the description of "Armageddon" so loosely, I felt we all needed another reminder of the events that must take place *before* we see the *real* Armageddon. More on that later.

And make no mistake about it, there will be more wars. Not all of them are identified through prophecy, so we shouldn't try looking for them all. WWI and WWII cannot be pinpointed in the scriptures. Yet they played a major role in the rebirth of the nation of Israel. You can be sure the Gulf War and the War on Terrorism will also be recorded as playing a significant role in Israel's future. And unfortunately, Russia's unprovoked war on Ukraine is presently threatening to draw Europe, the US, NATO and others into another dangerous situation where the "N" word has been revived. Even more trouble follows Israel into its future. Later chapters (6 and 14) will describe two major wars that will involve Israel.

5) *Jews Returning to Israel*

"And I will bring them out from the peoples and gather them from the countries and bring them to their own land; and I will feed them on the mountains of Israel, by the streams, and in all the inhabited places of the land."   (Ezekiel 34:13)

Israel was revived as a nation in May of 1948, an historic phenomenon. It had ceased being an independent nation ever since the Babylonian captivity in 606 BC. From that point forward, it ceased to be a sovereign nation. From 606 BC to 70 AD it was always under foreign domination either by the Babylonians, Persians, or Romans. After the Romans forced the Jews out of their land, they were scattered throughout the world until the early 1900's when they began returning to their homeland, culminating in a declaration of nationhood in 1948. That's over 2,500 years from the Babylonian captivity to 1948! No other people or nation has ever experienced such a miraculous rebirth.

The world is now focused on the Jews returning from all over the world. Their focus is not so much the amazement of fulfilled prophecy, but simply the rarity of this kind of story. A race, a nation, a religion, a language all returning to a home that's been occupied for centuries by others -- Egyptians, Greeks, Romans, Arabs, Turks, British.... Yet as we all know, conflict with their Arab neighbors and those claiming the same land is headlines news. This will be a constant thorn of contention with which the world must grapple. This birth of a new nation was the focus of Christ's response to a question He was asked "...Tell us, when will these things be and what will be the sign of Your coming, and of the end of the age?"

(Matthew 24:3)

Christ answered by describing many signs (false christs, wars and rumors of wars, famines, pestilences and earthquakes) after which He explained "All these are the beginning of birth pangs" (vs 8). Then He went on in vs. 32 to tie these signs to a parable as another means for those who would be living at that momentous time in history when He would return, to recognize the nearness of His coming:

"Now learn the parable from the fig tree: when its branch has already become tender and puts forth its leaves, you know that

6

summer is near; so, you too, when you see all these things, recognize that he is near, right at the door. Truly I say to you, this generation will not pass away until all these things take place."

(Matthew 24:32-34)

We have two things to consider here. First, that the parable is about a fig tree that signals summer is near, similar to the way He said the signs were like birth pangs (vs 32) pointing to the soon arrival of a baby. When you see the signs, then summer, birth, or His Coming is near.

Second, He uses the fig tree, which in Scripture usually refers to the nation of Israel. By doing this He is being even more specific. He is saying that when you see these signs, the fig tree-Israel- will be blossoming, and you will have a reference from which to measure His next statement: "this generation will not pass away until all these things take place." Since we have the date of May 1948 when the fig tree, Israel, blossomed as a nation, we know "these things" which are yet to "take place" (all the events related to the rise of Antichrist and the persecution of Jews and Christians as well as the judgments on all mankind as described in verses 9-31) will be seen by *the generation that saw Israel be birthed as a nation.* In broad terms that means any living remnant of those living during that major event in history, 1948. That includes babies at age 1 to adults at age 101.

Scholars debate over what is a generation. Is it 40, 80, or 100 years? I believe it simply means all those living at that time- *a generation*. Our Lord did not want to set a date anyone could calculate. Matthew 24:36 clearly says, "But of that day and hour no one knows, not even the angels, nor the Son, but the Father alone."

All He wanted us to know is the age in which this would occur. *And that age is now upon us.* Everyone living in May 1948, I believe is part of a generation that "will not pass away" until we see our Lord's return. Babies that were alive back then have a long life ahead of them that could easily be projected to 70-80-90 years. Therefore, we *might* have until around 2038 or thereabouts.

All this is strong evidence that points to our generation being the *last generation*. I seriously hope you will watch for the rest of the evidence that points to the very same thing throughout this book.

Chapter 2

Amazing Prophecies
Already Fulfilled

"And so we have the prophetic word made more sure, to which you do well to pay attention as to a lamp shining in a dark place, until the day dawns and the morning star arises in your hearts. But know this first of all, that no prophecy of Scripture is a matter of one's own interpretation for no prophecy was ever made by an act of human will, but men moved by the Holy Spirit spoke from God."

(2 Peter 1:19-21)

More scientists, sociologists, and other professionals are getting into the business of prophecy. The mystery and intrigue that surrounds predictions for the future attracts people from all walks of life. We all want to know what is going to happen before it actually does. There is a god-like power in having this kind of knowledge. It's like being inside on the planning. It's also a strong confirmation that there is a divine being behind the scenes trying to warn us and teach us through such prophecies.

You can take all of the voices down through history that claimed to be prophetic and you'll have nothing more than an overrated cheap movie, good for a few exciting scenes. And if you look at the substance, the benefit, the consistency of such predictions, you'll find them hollow. They have no grand purpose, no divine origin, and do not pass the acid test of a prophet and prophecy:

"But know this first of all, that no prophecy of Scripture is a matter of one's own interpretation, for no prophecy was ever made by an act of human will, but men moved by the Holy Spirit spoke from God."   (2 Peter 1:20, 21)

"And you may say in your heart, `How shall we know the word which the Lord has not spoken?' When a prophet speaks in the name of the Lord, if the thing does not come about or come true, that is the thing which the Lord has not spoken. The prophet has spoken it presumptuously; you shall not be afraid of him."

(Deuteronomy 18:21, 22)

Biblical prophecy spans recorded history from the time of Adam, cir. 4,000 BC, and Abraham, cir. 2,000 BC, up through 100 AD when Christ's disciples were penning the visions of the last days. Bible scholars record hundreds of prophecies that have already been fulfilled, with many still remaining.

Since this book will focus on coming events that can be seen and recorded, I believe it is essential that we list a few of the prophecies that have already occurred. This will demonstrate to us the validity and divine nature of these ancient prophecies, as they once unfolded a couple of thousand years ago, and hopefully build a base of credibility and confidence in the Bible's prophetic words.

Prophecies concerning the Messiah or Savior of mankind are the most amazing since there were so many of them, covering a wide variety of details. Although there are over 300 references to the Messiah, scholars easily identify over 60 major Old Testament prophecies fulfilled when Jesus Christ of Nazareth was born and completed His mission. The odds of one person satisfying all 60 of these prophecies has been calculated to be more than 1 to 10^{157} (that's 1 with 157 zeros!).[1]

The first six prophecies illustrated here are samples of these 60 major Messianic prophecies. The other two prophecies cover other amazing events. All of these Old Testament prophecies were written centuries (1000 BC – 400BC) before they were fulfilled.

1) **PROPHECY**: "Therefore the Lord Himself will give you a sign: Behold, a virgin will be with child and bear a son, and she will call His name Immanuel (God with us)."   (Isaiah 7:14)

FULFILLMENT: "...and she was found to be with child by the Holy Spirit. And Joseph arose from his sleep and did as the angel of the Lord commanded him and took her as his wife and kept her

11

a virgin until she gave birth to a Son; and he called His name Jesus." (Matthew 1:18, 24, 25)

2) **PROPHECY**: "I will surely tell of the decree of the Lord: He said to Me `Thou art My Son, Today I have begotten Thee.'"

(Psalms 2:7)

FULFILLMENT: "...and behold, a voice out of the heavens, saying, 'This is My beloved Son, in whom I am well pleased.'"

(Matthew 3:7)

3) **PROPHECY**: "But as for you, Bethlehem Ephrathah, too little to be among the clans of Judah, from you One will go forth for Me to be ruler in Israel. His goings forth are from long ago, from the days of eternity." (Micah 5:2)

FULFILLMENT: "...Jesus was born in Bethlehem of Judea..."

(Matthew 2:1)

4) **PROPHECY**: "...Because He poured out Himself to death, and was numbered with the transgressors..." (Isaiah 53:12)

FULFILLMENT: "At that time two robbers were crucified with Him, one on the right and one on the left." (Matthew 27:38)

5) **PROPHECY**: Thirty pieces of silver are predicted to play a role in the Lord's death. "And I said to them, 'if it is good in your sight, give me my wages; but if not, never mind.' So they weighed out thirty shekels of silver as my wages. Then the Lord said to me,

'Throw it to the potter, that magnificent price at which I was valued by them.' So I took the thirty shekels of silver and threw them to the potter in the house of the Lord." (Zechariah 11:12, 13)

FULFILLMENT: All three of the elements of this prophecy are fulfilled when Judas betrays Jesus to the high priests:

° God's son is valued at 30 pieces of silver when the priests decide to give them to Judas:

"Then one of the twelve named Judas Iscariot, went to the chief priests and said, 'What are you willing to give me to deliver Him up to you?' And they weighed out to him thirty pieces of silver." (Matthew 26:14, 15)

° Thirty pieces cast down in the temple:

"Then when Judas...saw that He had been condemned, he felt remorse and returned the thirty pieces of silver to the chief priests and elders, saying, 'I have sinned by betraying innocent blood.' But they said, `What is that to us? See to that yourself.' And he threw the pieces of silver into the sanctuary and departed..." (Matthew 27:3-5)

° Priests kept the silver and bought a potter's field:

"And the chief priests took the pieces of silver and said, `It is not lawful to put them into the temple treasury, since it is the price of blood.' And they counseled together and with the money bought the potter's field as a burial place for strangers."

(Matthew 27:6-7)

COMMENT: This amazing prophecy is given by Zechariah during the 5th century BC. It was a type of prophecy that Jesus had no way of controlling. While many doubters will try to explain away prophecies as manipulated events by Christ so as to fulfill written prophecies, they cannot do that here. This prophecy, as well as many others, happened to Christ without any possibility of manipulation.

6) **PROPHECY**: The timing of the Messiah's appearance is given to Daniel during his exile in Babylon in the 5th century BC. He is told in a vision that 483 years would elapse from the time of a proclamation to help the Jews, who had already returned from Babylonian captivity back to Israel to rebuild their walls, and the time of the coming Messiah:

"So you are to know and discern that from the issuing of a decree to restore and rebuild Jerusalem until Messiah the Prince, there will be seven weeks (of years) and sixty-two weeks (of years); it will be built again, with plaza and moat...Then after the sixty-two weeks (of years) the Messiah will be cut off and have nothing..." (Daniel 9:25, 26)

14

FULFILLMENT: Cyrus, King of Persia, had already allowed many Jewish exiles to return to Israel after his defeat of the Babylonians in 539 BC. And the temple had already been rebuilt under the direction of Zerubbabel from 522-486 BC. In 445 BC Artaxerxes allowed Nehemiah and Ezra to also return to Israel to lead the rebuilding of the walls:

"And it came about in the month Nisan, in the 20th year of King Artaxerxes (445 BC)... the King said to me, `What would be your request?'...And I said to the King, `If it please the King, and if your servant has found favor before you, send me to Judah, to the city of my father's tombs, that I may rebuild it".

(Nehemiah 2: 1-5)

COMMENT: With this key date of 445 BC, we are told to expect 483 years to pass before the Messiah will be cut off. The usual date for Jesus' death is at 32 AD. The period from 445 BC to 32 AD is only 476 years (not the 483 years predicted). But our years have 365 days, while a prophetic year has 360 days. When you consider the difference (explained further in the next chapter) you get precisely the 483 years to when the Messiah was cut off. [2]

7) **PROPHECY**: "...and I will send to Nebuchadnezzar king of Babylon, My servant, and will bring them against this land

(Israel)... And this whole land shall be a desolation and a horror, and these nations shall serve the King of Babylon seventy years."   (Jeremiah 25:9, 11)

FULFILLMENT: "...Therefore He brought up against them the King of the Chaldeans... they burned the house of God, and broke down the wall of Jerusalem... and those who escaped from the sword he carried away to Babylon... All the days of its desolation it kept Sabbath until seventy years were complete."

(II Chronicles 36:17-21)

COMMENT: Jeremiah spoke his prophecies to the nation of Israel around 626 BC. Nebuchadnezzar stormed Jerusalem around 606 BC, taking the nation captive until around 536 BC. Archaeology and ancient history confirm these events. (Isaiah prophesied the same events in Isaiah 39:5-7, and he wrote his prophecies from 740 BC - 680 BC)

8) **PROPHECY**: Moses described two major national events in Israel's history.

(1) A mighty nation would invade, destroy and take captives: "The Lord will bring a nation against you from afar... it will eat the offspring of your herd and the produce of your ground until you are destroyed... And it shall besiege you in all your towns until your high and fortified walls in which you trusted come down..."

(Deuteronomy 28:49-52)

16

2) Israel will be destroyed again and scattered to global dispersion, even as some are sold as in ships... And there you shall offer slaves on ships to Egypt: "Moreover the Lord will scatter you among all peoples, from one end of the earth to the other end of the earth; and there you shall serve other gods, wood and stone... And among those nations you shall find no rest, and there shall be no resting place for the sole of your foot; but there the Lord will give you a trembling heart... And the Lord will bring you back to Egypt yourselves for sale to your enemies as male and female slaves..."   (Deuteronomy 28: 64-68)

FULLFILLMENT:

(1) Israel is destroyed by Babylon in 606 BC. 2 Chronicles 36: 17-21, describes the fulfillment of this prophecy.

(2) Israel is destroyed again and scattered in 70 AD when Titus attacks Jerusalem during the Roman Empire. The Romans also carried many of them off to Egypt to be sold into slavery. History shows how the Jews have been scattered and persecuted ever since. They were without a land and a nation for all those years from 70 AD to 1948 AD. Their safe return is the subject of volumes of other prophecies *being fulfilled at this very moment.*

COMMENT: Moses delivered these grave warnings to his people in the plains of Moab around 1260 BC just before his death and their entrance into the promised land. It was divine

17

warning, describing the curses and blessings that Israel could choose from. Their history has served as sort of a microcosm of all mankind. As mankind continued to sin and suffer the misery of discipline and its consequences, he also repeatedly received deliverance and restoration in order to draw him to repentance.

Chapter 3

Seven Years of Trouble

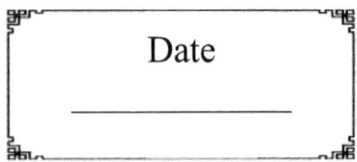

Date

_____

"...And he will make a covenant with the many for one week..."

(Daniel 9:27)

This is one of the most remarkable date-setting prophecies in the Bible. The first part of this prophecy predicts 69 weeks (seven-year periods) of judgment and trouble for the Jews because of their transgressions. Then one last week (seven years) is identified separately since it begins long after the 69 weeks have ended. Look at what the whole prophecy says, and then we'll look at the historical fulfillment.

"Seventy weeks have been decreed for your people and your holy city, to finish the transgression, to make an end of sin, to make atonement for iniquity, to bring in everlasting righteousness, to seal up vision and prophecy, and to anoint the most holy place. So you

19

are to know and discern that from the issuing of a decree to restore and rebuild Jerusalem until Messiah the Prince there will be seven weeks and sixty-two weeks; it will be built again, with plaza and moat, even in times of distress. Then after the sixty-two weeks the Messiah will be cut off and have nothing, and the people of the prince who is to come will destroy the city and sanctuary. And its end will come with a flood; even to the end will be war; desolations are determined. And he will make a firm covenant with the many for one week, but in the middle of the week he will put a stop to sacrifice and grain offering; and on the wing of abominations will come one who makes desolate, even until a complete destruction, one that is decreed, is poured out on the one who makes desolate."

(Daniel 9:24-27)

As Josh McDowel explains in his book *Evidence that Demands a Verdict*, "the Hebrew word for `week' is *shabua* and literally means a `seven'. Then, in Hebrew, the idea of 70 weeks is `seventy sevens'. [1]

In his book, McDowel gives a scholarly explanation as to the dating of these events described by Daniel. It leaves no doubt of the accuracy of this prophecy. Keep in mind that Daniel, himself a Jew, lived during the Babylonian exile of the Jews, 606 BC- 536 BC, a 70-year period of captivity, itself a fulfillment of one of Jeremiah's prophecies. (Jeremiah 25:9, 11) (This 70-years of exile is not to be confused with the 70 weeks of years (490 years) of future judgment spoken of in Daniel's prophecy. Seventy just seems to be one of God's favorite numbers when it comes to discipline.)

The 70 weeks of years (490 years) was to begin when the decree was given to "restore and rebuild Jerusalem". Nehemiah, one of the Jews in exile, sought the Lord in prayer and got King Artaxerxes' approval to start the work in 445 BC (Nehemiah 2:1-8). And the end of the 69 weeks of years (483 years) was described as "until Messiah the Prince is cut off". The crucifixion of Jesus Christ took place in 32 AD (some say 30 AD).

According to McDowel, and other Biblical Scholars, historical and prophetic references to a year considers 12 months of 30 days or 360 days. The 69 weeks of years would then be equivalent to 69 weeks x 7 years x 360 days, or 173,880 days.

In terms of our calendar, 445 BC to 32 AD is equivalent to 476 years or 173,740 days (476 x 365 days = 173,740).[2] When you consider leap year days, and the difference in the exact month these events occurred, you realize this prophecy has proven itself accurate. A period of exactly 483 years elapsed. Which means the only remaining part of the prophecy to be fulfilled is one last week -- *seven years*.

In fact, Charles Dyer says emphatically in his book, *The Rise of Babylon,* that "the day Christ rode into Jerusalem to proclaim Himself Israel's Messiah was exactly 483 years to the day after the command to restore and rebuild Jerusalem had been given." [3]

When the Jews crucified their Messiah in 32 AD, yelling "crucify him", the prophetic clock stopped. *One week of seven years still remains.* This is very important to remember.

Our hint of when this last seven-year period begins is given by Daniel when he says, "And he will make a firm covenant with the many for one week..." Since this last week is to represent Israel's last stage of experiencing the purpose of this prophecy, ("...make an end to sin, to make atonement for iniquity, to bring in everlasting righteousness, to seal up vision and prophecy, and to anoint the most holy place...") a multitude of things will be happening.

The Jews will mistakenly make a peace agreement with a smooth-talking world leader. They will actually consider him their Messiah, the "he" in Daniel 9:27. And this same "he" is the Antichrist talked about in Revelation, where all of the tribulations that accompany his reign are described in detail. Take a quick glance at just some of the things that will be happening during this period:

"...over a fourth of the earth, to kill with sword and famine and with pestilence and by the wild beasts of the earth."

(Revelation 6:8)

"...I saw underneath the altar the souls of those who had been slain because of the testimony which they had maintained."

(Revelation 6:9)

22

"...and there was a great earthquake; and the sun became black as sackcloth made of hair, and the whole moon became as blood."

(Revelation 6:12)

"...and the stars of the sky fell to the earth, as a fig tree casts its unripe figs when shaken by a great wind."   (Revelation 6:13)

"...and there came hail and fire, mixed with blood... and a third of the earth was burnt up, and a third of the trees were burnt up, and all the green grass was burnt up."   (Revelation 8:7)

"...and something like a great mountain burning with fire was thrown into the sea; and a third of the sea became blood."

(Revelation 8:8)

"...and he opened the bottomless pit; and smoke went up out of the pit, like the smoke of a great furnace; ...out of the smoke came forth locusts... and they were not permitted to kill anyone, but to torment for five months..."   (Revelation 9:2-5)

"...and the number of the armies of the horseman was 200 million; I heard the number of them...the riders had breastplates the color of fire and of hyacinth and of brimstone; and the heads of the horses are like the heads of lions; and out of their mouths proceed fire and smoke and brimstone."   (Revelation 9:16-17)

"...A third of mankind was killed by these plagues, by the fire and the smoke and the brimstone, which proceeded out of their mouths."   (Revelation 9:18)

And much more is recorded to occur during this time. Even if you've read about these things before, it is a disturbing picture to visualize. It seems as if all hell has broken loose, with natural disasters, and mankind in total anarchy. And that's just what happens.

Whether you are at a point in your life to see the truth of these scriptures or not, they will prove themselves out. But if you wish to really see God's overall purpose behind these horrible events, consider this.

Man still has a choice throughout this entire ordeal. He can choose to suffer either Satan's wrath for not accepting the "mark of the beast" (more on this in Chapter 9) and be killed; or suffer the wrath of God for receiving the mark and joining Antichrist's system (Revelation 14:11).

The Antichrist chooses to blaspheme God. That's only one of the many reasons you cannot allow yourself to become part of his system. "And he opened his mouth in blasphemies against God, to blaspheme His name and His tabernacle, that is, those who dwell in

24

heaven." (Revelation 13:6)

Also, as you consider what your choice would be if you are still here when these things occur, here's more.

In Matthew 10:28 we are told: "And do not fear those who kill the body but are unable to kill the soul; but rather fear Him who is able to destroy both soul and body in hell."

Natural disasters, armies, and Satan (through his Antichrist) can kill the body. But the Lord can go beyond that. He will call the final judgment on our souls. "It is a terrifying thing to fall into the hands of the living God." (Hebrews 10:31)

We all too often do not understand how a God of love can also be a God of judgment. Whether we understand this or not, it is God's character; He is also a "consuming fire". (Hebrews 12:29)

So, as we understand clearly what our choices are, look again at the situation as God sees it:

"And the rest of mankind, who were not killed by these plagues, did not repent of the works of their hands, so as not to worship demons, and the idols of gold and of silver and of brass and of stone and of wood, which can neither see nor hear nor walk; and *they did not repent* of their murders nor of their sorceries nor of their immorality nor of their thefts." (Revelation 9:20, 21)

25

Mankind continues to worship his gold, possessions, and humanistic and false religions even as heaven breaks forth with supernatural judgments: "...and men blasphemed God because of the plague of the hail, because its plague was extremely severe".

(Revelation 16:21)

God continues to hope that man will repent, and simply say "I'm sorry. Forgive me. I see how I've been all wrong. I admit you are the Lord. And I will do it your way from now on, even if it means death from all those who still oppose you."

And here is a very comforting promise for all those who do repent, whether you wait until this seven-year period arrives, or wisely do it now. Believers *never* experience the wrath of God! Although we may suffer trouble of all kinds, none of it will be personally directed at us as God's wrath. He has promised us that:

"Because you have kept the word of My perseverance, I also will keep you from the hour of testing, that hour which is about to come upon the whole world, to test those who dwell upon the earth."   (Revelation 3:10)

"Much more then, having now been justified by His blood, we shall be saved from the wrath of God through Him."

(Romans 5:9)

"He who believes in the Son has eternal life; but he who does not obey the Son shall not see life, but the wrath of God abides on him." (John 3:36)

God's promise to save us from His wrath becomes particularly important when scholars try to pinpoint the time of the Rapture and Resurrection of believers. As this chapter described this special 7-year period of tribulation for the Jews, we also know that the saints, followers of Christ, will also be the target of this antichrist and there will be many martyrs. And since it will be shown in other chapters that Gods' wrath will also be poured out during this time, the real challenge is to understand the time frame of when this wrath begins. For when it begins, the saints (Jews and Gentiles) will be gone. The great escape of His wrath will have taken place. And as you may know, there are many who believe this escape, the Rapture, will take place before this 7-year period and others who believe it will occur around the middle of the 7-year period. I will eagerly discuss the strongest points for both of these major positions in Chapter 8: The Resurrection and Rapture.

Dark days are coming. It will be the "hour of trial" for mankind. You and your family must be informed of these things before they overtake you.

Chapter 4

Europe Takes Charge

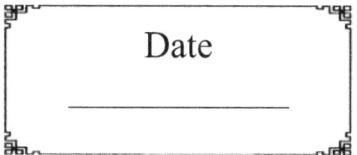

Date

_____

"...And the ten horns which you saw are ten kings, who have not yet received a kingdom, but they receive authority as kings with the beast (Antichrist) for one hour. These have one purpose, and they give power and authority to the beast (Antichrist)."

(Revelation 17:12, 13)

It was in the planning for decades, and formally achieved on January 1, 1993. The old Roman Empire, comprised of European nations, prominent from 300 BC through 476 AD, was revived and established as the new European Union (EU).

This is a very significant event in the prophetic clock, since as this chapter will show, this revived Roman Empire is the world power that the Antichrist uses to gain world support for his deceptive plans to bring peace to the world.

First let's look at the prophecy given through a dream to King Nebuchadnezzar of Babylon in the 6th century BC. Daniel the prophet was there in exile to help give the interpretation of the meaning of a large statue that the king saw in his dream:

"You, O King, were looking and behold, there was a single great statue; that statue, which was large and of extraordinary splendor, was standing in front of you, and its appearance was awesome. The head of that statue was made of fine gold, its breast and its arms of silver, its belly and its thighs of bronze, its legs of iron, its feet partly of iron and partly of clay. You continued looking until a stone was cut out without hands, and it struck the statue on its feet of iron and clay and crushed them. Then the iron, the clay, the bronze, the silver and the gold were crushed all at the same time and became like chaff from the summer threshing floors; and the wind carried them away so that not a trace of them was found. But the stone that struck the statue became a great mountain and filled the whole earth. This was the dream; now we shall tell its interpretation before the king."   (Daniel 2:31-36)

After summarizing the dream, Daniel explains the meaning of this amazing prophecy, which centers on world empires that would rise to prominence in the future. Look at what this godly servant, Daniel, told Nebuchadnezzar and the rest of mankind what this statue meant:

> "...You (Nebuchadnezzar) are the head of gold. And after you there will arise another kingdom inferior to you, then another third kingdom of bronze, which will rule over all the earth. Then there will be a fourth kingdom as strong as iron; inasmuch as iron crushes and shatters all things, so, like iron that breaks in pieces, it will crush and break all these in pieces. And in that you saw the feet and toes, partly of potter's clay and partly of iron, it will be a divided kingdom; but it will have in it the toughness of iron, inasmuch as you saw the iron mixed with common clay. And as the toes of the feet were partly of iron and partly of pottery, so some of the kingdom will be strong and part of it will be brittle. And in that you saw the iron mixed with common clay, they will combine with one another in the seed of men; but they will not adhere to one another, even as iron does not combine with pottery. And in the days of those kings the God of heaven will set up a kingdom which will never be destroyed, and that kingdom will not be left for another people; it will crush and put an end to all these kingdoms, but it will itself endure forever. Inasmuch as you saw that a stone was cut out of the mountain without hands and that it crushed the iron, the bronze, the clay, the silver, and the gold, the great God has made known to the king what will take place in the future; so the dream is true, and its interpretation is trustworthy."

(Daniel 2:38-45)

Daniel did not know the names of the future kingdoms, but we now know them as: Babylonian (626-539 BC) – the head of gold;

the Medo-Persian (539-331 BC) – the breasts and arms of silver; the Greek (331-323 BC) – the belly and thighs of bronze; and the Roman (300 BC- 476 AD) – the legs of iron and feet of iron and clay.[1] The divided kingdom made of iron and clay, represented by *ten* toes, is the Roman Empire that lost its power when it divided into separate smaller nations.

After explaining the meaning of the statue, Daniel then tells the king about what amounts to the final victory of God's coming Kingdom. The vision describes a stone, cut from a mountain, that crushes this last kingdom. That stone is Christ, when He comes to set up His Kingdom on earth.

Daniel's amazing prophecy gives us an overall picture of the major events. As we view the EU today, something else must happen to the Old Roman Empire. As it strengthens, it will be composed of *ten* nations (the *ten* toes, and *ten* horns referenced earlier) or *ten* regions. I like what Dr. David Jeremiah says in his book, *Escape the Coming Night:* "The Bible indicates this Revived Roman Empire will have ten heads and yet the European Common Market has fifteen countries at this time. It does not matter how many there are now, the time will come when there will be just ten. God's Word is inerrantly accurate."[2] Dr. Jeremiah wrote this in 2001, more than 20 years ago. And right now, the EU has a 27-nation alliance. This now becomes an issue to watch as it comes into focus as a world leader by way of some sort of 10-nation/region

31

alliance.

To give further support to this prophecy, later Daniel has a dream of his own and we are told more through the use of four great beasts: a lion, a bear, a leopard, and a terrifying beast with *ten* horns. (Daniel 7:1-8)

The uncanny accuracy of these prophecies should be enough to astound the hardest skeptic. In this prophecy Daniel describes the third beast as a "leopard". We already know this refers to the Greek empire, as Daniel's interpretation of Nebuchadnezzar's dream and history bear out. But in this dream, the leopard had four heads, identifying it even more since we know that "following Alexander's death, the Greek empire broke into four parts, just as Daniel had predicted. Macedonia and Greece, Alexander's original empire, went to Cassandra. Lysimachus grabbed Thrace and Asia Minor. Palestine and Egypt went to Ptolemy I; and Syria, Mesopotamia, and Medio-Persia went to Seleucus I."[3]

The fourth beast mentioned by Daniel in this seventh chapter, was called a "terrifying beast...with *ten* horns." This terrifying beast (EU) has now formed. Keep your eyes on it and mark the dates of its growth and development. But be comforted with its prophetic destiny:

> "I kept looking, and that horn was waging war with the saints and
> overpowering them until the Ancient of Days came, and judgment
> was passed in favor of the saints of the Highest One, and the time

32

arrived when the saints took possession of the kingdom."

(Daniel 7:21-23)

As we view the world today, post global pandemic, with Russia, China and Iran rattling their sabers, it appears that the EU is weaker than it needs to be. This is all the more reason to watch for how and when things change as the prophetic comes into focus.

The fourth beast will be a cruel empire, crushing the earth. Perhaps its combined military and economic strength will give it the power needed to wield such commanding influence. Yet the "Ancient of Days", will pass judgment and give the saints the victory.

Chapter 5

Antichrist Brokers Israeli Peace Treaty

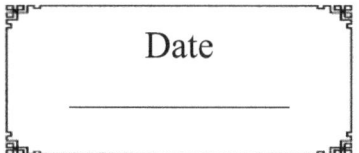

Date
_____

"...And he will make a firm covenant with the many for one week..."

(Daniel 9:27)

W e have already focused on the "one week" or seven-year period that marks the end of this age. Now let's look closely at the leader that walks onto the scene (the "he" in the above scripture) and remarkably gains the world's attention and confidence to bring about peace and order to a troubled world. When we recognize this great deceiver, and see him propose this agreement, we'll have a very significant turning point to record.

The revived Roman Empire, identified earlier as the new European Union (EU), will be the political stage for this leader. Read what Daniel says:

"After this I kept looking in the night visions, and behold, a fourth beast, dreadful and terrifying and extremely strong; and it had large iron teeth. It devoured and crushed and trampled down the remainder with its feet; and it was different from all the beasts that were before it, and it had ten horns. While I was contemplating the horns, behold, another horn, a little one, came up among them, and three of the first horns were pulled out by the roots before it; and behold, this horn possessed eyes like the eyes of a man, and a mouth uttering great boasts." (Daniel 7:7-8)

The "little horn" represents a king or leader from this ten-nation federation. He is for some reason smaller, perhaps because of the nation he represents or his lack of exposure to the public. Regardless, he witnesses the removal of three others as "three of the first horns were pulled out by the roots before it". Something close to expulsion will happen to three of its member countries.

All kinds of probable scenarios could be presented in order to explain how the leader of the EU will have any need, or opportunity, to make an agreement with Israel. But in the arena of new world politics, we can easily see how any leader with charisma and power could galvanize the world's attention by developing a peace plan for the Middle East crisis. It could happen in any number of ways. It's not my purpose to try and guess, but to alert you on how to identify this leader when he is revealed.

But before I go on to describe other characteristics and

35

prophecies regarding this leader, keep in mind that the seven-year agreement we read about comes from *divine prophecy*. We know that it will last only three and a half years as he breaks it midway (see chapter 13 for more details on this event).

Of course, by now you recognize this leader is the infamous Antichrist, the so-called world hero so desperately needed. Let's look at some other references to him to get a better picture.

"Here is wisdom. Let him who has understanding calculate the number of the beast, for the number is that of a man; and his number is six hundred and sixty-six." (Revelation 13:18)

"And he opened his mouth in blasphemies against God, to blaspheme His name and His tabernacle, that is, those who dwell in heaven." (Revelation 13:6)

"And it was given to him to make war with the saints and to overcome them; and authority over every tribe and people and tongue and nation was given to him." (Revelation 13:7)

"...and he will destroy to an extraordinary degree... He will destroy mighty men and the holy people." (Daniel 8:24)

"I kept looking, and that horn was waging war with the saints and overpowering them."   (Daniel 7:21)

"Then the king will do as he pleases, and he will exalt and magnify himself above every god and will speak monstrous things against the God of gods; and he will prosper until the indignation is finished, for that which is decreed will be done."

(Daniel 11:36)

"...that is, the one whose coming is in accord with the activity of Satan, with all power and signs and false wonders, and with all the deception of wickedness for those who perish, because they did not receive the love of the truth so as to be saved. And for this reason, God will send upon them a deluding influence so that they might believe what is false, in order that they all may be judged who did not believe the truth but took pleasure in wickedness."

(2 Thessalonians 2:9-12)

What a great world hero he will be! But that is what deception is all about. It means you are fooled, tricked, or naive to trust in false claims. But now, you have been warned. Be on the alert so that you will not be deluded and take pleasure in following this leader's deceptive plan to save Israel, then destroy it.

Chapter 6

Israel at War with Russia

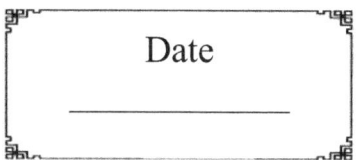

Date

_____

"After many days you will be summoned; in the latter years you will come into the land that is restored from the sword, whose inhabitants have been gathered from many nations to the mountains of Israel which had been a continual waste; but its people were brought out from the nations, and they are living securely, all of them. And you will go up, you will come like a storm; you will be like a cloud covering the land, you and all your troops, and many peoples with you."   (Ezekiel 38:8, 9)

Despite the decades of effort by leaders and nations to find the eternally elusive "peaceful solution to the Middle East crisis", Israel will finally reach a level of peace! At first, all the extraordinary efforts to bring peace to Israel will bear fruit. A major peace treaty will be signed, and the nation will sigh a great relief. But while they are living "securely" under this arrangement, a "cloud" of troops will attack. We're going to look at the prophecies that describe the circumstances that lead up to this attack. We'll also learn who it will be, and how they are soundly defeated.

When the United Nations attacked Iraq on January 16, 1991, the newspapers expressed the public's fears and confusion as they wondered, "Is this going to be the so-called Armageddon?" And again, as I've already mentioned, On Oct 6, 2022, President Joe Biden exclaimed similar fear. They will probably be asking the same ignorant question about every threatening war from now until the real Armageddon, including the war I'm about to describe. None of them fit the description of the infamous Armageddon. And you'll see why as we set the stage and identify the players in this war.

Please keep in mind there always exists the possibility of other battles or wars to occur before this one. The Gulf War with Iraq (1991) was not specifically prophesied; nor was WW I, WW II, or the War on Terrorism specifically prophesied. None of them were identified specifically in scriptures. *But this one is prophesied* throughout the scriptures, and we need to be on the lookout for it. This fuse once lit, will lead the world into a campaign of battles that explode into the real Armageddon.

WHEN IS THIS WAR AGAINST ISRAEL

Do you remember how the opening verse states that Israel would be "living securely"? When will Israel ever have that blessed pleasure? Ever since her rebirth as a nation in May of 1948, she has been under constant threat of extinction. It will surely be a rare experience for her to be living securely. Surely we will be able to recognize this when it happens. Another verse, Ezekiel 38:11, adds even more when it describes Israel as "...the land of unwalled villages...who are at rest, that live securely, all of them living without walls, having no bars or gates..."

Clearly, this time of rest referenced in these verses refer to a time *just after* Israel signs a peace treaty and proudly proclaims her victory. But little does she realize, this treaty will usher in hard times; very, very hard times.

This treaty starts the seven-year period called the Tribulation, the last years given to Israel to bring this age of history to its close: "And he will make a firm covenant with many for one week (seven years) ..."   (Daniel 9:27)

WHO MAKES THE PEACE TREATY

The same verses tell us it will be a Roman prince that makes this treaty with Israel. When Daniel prophesies about Israel's last seventy weeks (70 x 7 years), he records a special event describing the killing of their Messiah (Jesus Christ in 32 AD). He says that the people of the "prince who is to come" destroy the city of Jerusalem. History records that Romans destroyed Jerusalem in 70 AD.

40

Therefore, the prince who is yet to come is a Roman:

"Then after sixty-two weeks the Messiah will be cut off and have nothing, and the people of the prince *who is to come* will destroy the city and the sanctuary...And he will make a firm covenant with the many for one week (seven years) ..."   (Daniel 9:26,27)

Most all Bible scholars agree that this Roman leader will come from the revived Roman Empire recently formed called the European Union. This new alliance of nations in Europe will produce a leader that will come to the rescue of Israel. This is why Israel is described as living securely since this European alliance will develop a strong reputation as a warrior: "Who is like the beast (Antichrist) and who is able to wage war with him?"

(Revelation 13:4)

WHO DARES TO ATTACK

The Antichrist will establish himself in the eyes of the world as a powerful world leader, showing everyone how the "new world order" should work:

"And in the latter period of their rule, when the transgressors have run their course, a king will arise insolent and skilled in intrigue. And his power will be mighty, but not by his own power (Satan's power), and he will destroy to an extraordinary degree and prosper and perform his will; he will destroy mighty men and the holy people. And through his shrewdness he will cause deceit to succeed by his influence; and he will destroy many while they are at ease. He will even oppose the Prince of Princes, but he will be broken without human agency." (Daniel 8:23:25)

This leader is actually able to destroy many by means of peace. (That's what the first white horse of the four horsemen of the apocalypse in Revelation 6 describes – a peaceful, deceitful leader.) It looks like sanctions are used as a viable weapon. Cutting off a nation from being able to trade with others is a powerful economic weapon to force cooperation.

With this kind of protection on Israel's side, who would dare to attack her? Whoever it is will usher in the fulfillment of the second horse of the apocalypse (war) identified in the seal judgments in Revelation:

"And when He broke the second seal, I heard the second living creature saying "Come." And another, a red horse, went out; and to him who sat on it, it was granted to take peace from the earth, and that men should slay one another; and a great sword was given to him." (Revelation 6:3-4)

So who will initiate this aggression against Israel? The prophets, Daniel and Ezekiel, give us the clues as they each describe events that unfold towards "the end times." Two battles come in rapid succession. One by "the king of the South"— Egypt; the other by "the king of the North"- Russia and its allies. A series of prophecies I will show describe these events. But one of the key verses that helps pull these two events together says,

"And at the end time the king of the South will collide with him, (the Antichrist) and the king of the North will storm against him with chariots, with horsemen, and with many ships; and he will enter countries, overflow them, and pass through."

(Daniel 11:40)

Here we see the last part of a prophecy given by Daniel concerning the rise and fall of kingdoms in the Middle East during the last five centuries BC, along with reference to the last ones during the end time. This verse tells of the "king of the South", "at the end time", as "colliding with *him.*" The king of the South is identified in the next few verses in Daniel, chapter 11, as Egypt. The nation colliding with Egypt, referred to as "him" in verse 40, is represented by the king who magnifies himself above every god and speaks monstrous things against God: the Antichrist. He will be leading the EU and "protecting" Israel.

43

"Then the king will do as he pleases, and he will exalt and magnify himself above every god and will speak monstrous things against the God of gods; and will prosper until the indignation is finished, for that which is decreed will be done. And he will show no regard for the gods of his fathers or for the desire of women, nor will he show regard for any other god; for he will magnify himself above them all."   (Daniel 11:36, 37)

The next few verses in this same prophecy give us some hints as to why Egypt and the EU collide:

"But instead, he will honor a god of fortresses, a god whom his fathers did not know; he will honor him with gold, silver, costly stones, and treasures. And he will take action against the strongest fortresses with the help of a foreign god; he will give great honor to those who acknowledge him, and he will cause them to rule over the many and will parcel out the land for a price."

(Daniel 11:38, 39)

The powerful new world leader gives praise to those nations acknowledging him and is empowered to give out land in exchange for a price. Perhaps this EU leader, who has recently arranged a peace treaty for Israel, is parceling out land to the Arab nations that cooperated. And perhaps Egypt is threatened when she sees a great change in the balance of power in the region. She may also be the target of sanctions by the EU in order to force her into compliance with the new seven-year treaty negotiated by the EU.

There of course could be any number of reasons for their disagreement during these turbulent times. It's not my place to figure out why these two powers will battle. I merely want to demonstrate any number of logical, plausible circumstances could precipitate such a battle. The point is, *they will clash.*

"Then he will stretch out his hand against other countries, and the land of Egypt will not escape. But he will gain control over the hidden treasures of gold and silver, and over all the precious things of Egypt; and the Libyans and Ethiopians will follow at his heels."   (Daniel 11:42, 43)

Egypt is defeated! The Antichrist gains control over their gold, silver, and other valuable assets, bringing Egypt to its economic knees. And then he sets his sights on Libya and Ethiopia – the African alliance.

Now let's go back to see what else Daniel has to say:

"And at the time the king of the South will collide with him, and the king of the North will storm against him with chariots, with horseman, and with many ships; and he will enter countries, overflow them, and pass through."   (Daniel 11:40)

The North identified in this prophecy is obviously not in accord with the way the EU and its leader has administered the new peace treaty protecting Israel. He's giving powers and lands away to those who support him. This clearly has an impact on the North (later we will identify Russia and her allies as this northern king), and the North takes the initiative to "storm against him."

This 40th verse in Daniel not only identifies this attack by Russia and her allies, but it continues to explain how the leader of the EU (continually referred to as "he") enters numerous countries and overtakes them. Russia takes advantage of all this activity and challenges the EU in some of these regions. Another prophecy in Ezekiel amplifies what Russia's real objective is when confronting the EU.

This "king of the North" wants Israel. They believe she is the source of all the conflict that plagues the world community. So, while this king attacks the EU in various places (Daniel 11:40), he also marches, mightily aligned with other countries, into Israel.

This prophecy given by Ezekiel fills in many more details about who this "king of the North" is and what happens to him and his allies in Israel. Read about those involved in this war.

"And the word of the Lord came to me saying, Son of Man, set your face toward Gog of the land of Magog, the prince of Rosh, Meshech, Tubal, and prophesy against him, and say, 'Thus says the Lord God, "Behold, I am against you, O Gog, prince of Rosh, Meshech, and Tubal. And I will turn you about, and put hooks into your jaws, and I will bring you out, and all your army, horses, and horsemen, all of them splendidly attired, a great company with buckler and shield, all of them wielding swords; Persia, Ethiopia, and Put with them, all of them with shield and helmet; Gomer with all its troops; Beth Togarmah from the remote parts of the north with all its troops -- many peoples with you.'"

(Ezekiel 38:1-6)

There are three groups that form this alliance referred to in Daniel as the "king of the North": 1) Gog of the land of Magog, the prince of Rosh, Meshech, and Tubal; 2) Persia, Ethiopia, and Put; and 3) Gomer and Beth-Togarmah.

These descriptions are given by Ezekiel, describing the peoples and nations by the names used during that era. Many of these names represent grandsons of Noah who settled their tribes in certain areas of the region. Magog, Meshech, Tubal, Put, Gomer, Togarmah, and Cush (translated in many Bibles as Ethiopia) were all grandsons and great grandsons of Noah (Genesis 10).

The first group is headed up by "Gog". There is no biblical

background for this word. It is only used twice: once here when referring to the leader of this alliance; and once again in Revelation 20. In both cases it refers to the *leader of the forces going against God's people*. In this case it also describes Gog as the prince of Rosh.

Rosh is the key to understanding where this leader comes from. Hal Lindsey, in his book "The Late Great Planet Earth", quotes German scholar Dr. Keil when he says of Rosh, "The Byzantine and Arabic writers frequently mention a people called Ros and Rus, dwelling in the country of Taurus, and reckoned among the Scythian tribes."[1]

Lindsey also quotes Bishop Lowth of England when he wrote "Rosh, taken as a proper name, in Ezekiel signifies the inhabitants of Scythia, from whom the modern Russians derive their name."[2]

Jewish historians and Hebrew scholars indicate that Magog settled in the northern regions above the Caucasus Mountains and that Meshech was the founder of Moshci, source of the name of Moscow.[3]

Tubal also settled near Meshech, to the east, making all three of these peoples the ancestors of the present-day Russians.

The second group that is allied with *Gog* is easily identified as Iran (Persia), Africa (Ethiopia or *Cush*), and Libya (*Put*).

Ethiopia is a translation of the Hebrew name, *Cush*, who was a grandson to Noah. The land of Cush cannot be limited to Ethiopia, since the Cushites were a black people who migrated to the Arabian Peninsula and south of Egypt. [4]

The same principle applies to the Hebrew word *Put* being translated as Libya. This descendant of Noah migrated to the land west of Egypt and became the roots of Libya, Tunisia, and Algeria. Therefore, northern Africa will form a part of this alliance. [5]

The third group, identified as *Gomer* and *Togarmah,* are also descendants of Noah's sons. Recent archaeological finds show that Gomer settled in the north of the Black Sea, then south and west into Europe. Josephus, a Jewish historian, places Gomer and his people in the area of Germany, Poland, and Czechoslovakia. [6]

Lindsey quotes Wilhelm Genesius, a Hebrew scholar from the early nineteenth century, concerning Togarmah: "They are a northern nation and country sprung from Gomer abounding in horses and mules." [7] The conclusion being Togarmah founded Armenia and is also part of the modern southern Russia and the Cossacks of eastern Russia. [8]

Let's take a breather from these old names. All of these nations named by their founding fathers (sons of Noah) surely make up a remarkable prophecy. Trying to identify them all is also a challenge I gladly leave up to the scholars of history. And discovering a plausible reason for each people group to join Gog is likewise a challenge. But neither is it at all necessary. Just watch as it unfolds and be even more convinced of the divine nature of this prophecy.

GOG'S DEFEAT

Now that we have examined the major participants in the king of the North's alliance, let's look at the details given in Ezekiel about his defeat. *Yes, his defeat.* One could hardly imagine how such a large force could be defeated. That's because it will be a supernatural event.

God is not happy with Gog's (*the leader of forces going against God's people*) idea to come against Israel with such destruction. He has other plans for this northern alliance. And these plans will be the answers to a nation's prayers when stunned by such an attack. Here is the full account:

"'And it will come about on the day, when Gog comes against the land of Israel', declares the Lord, 'that My fury will mount up in My anger. And in My zeal and My blazing wrath I will declare that on that day there will surely be a great earthquake in the land of Israel. And the fish of the sea, the birds of the heavens, the beasts of the field, all the creeping things that creep on the earth, and all the men who are on the face of the earth will shake at My presence; the mountains also will be thrown down, the steep pathways will collapse, and every wall will fall to the ground. And I shall call for a sword against him on all My mountains,' declares the Lord God. 'Every man's sword will be against his brother.

And with pestilence and with blood I shall enter into judgment with him; and I shall rain on him, and his troops, and on the many peoples who are with him, a torrential rain, with hailstones, fire, and brimstone. And I shall magnify Myself, sanctify Myself, and make Myself known in the sight of many nations; and they will know that I am the Lord. And you, son of man, prophesy against Gog, and say, 'Thus says the Lord God, Behold, I am against you, O Gog, prince of Rosh, Meshech, and Tubal; and I shall turn you around, drive you on, take you up from the remotest parts of the north, and bring you against the mountains of Israel. And I shall strike your bow from your left hand, and dash down your arrows from your right hand. You shall fall on the mountains of Israel, you and all your troops, and the peoples who are with you; I shall give you as food to every kind of predatory bird and beast of the field. You will fall on the open field; for it is I who have spoken,' declares the Lord God. And I shall send fire upon Magog and those who inhabit the coastlands in safety; and they will know that I am the Lord. And My holy name I shall make known in the midst of My people Israel; and I shall not let My holy name be profaned any more. And the nations will know that I am the Lord, the Holy one in Israel. Behold it is coming and it shall be done, declares the Lord God. That is the day of which I have spoken. Then those who inhabit the cities of Israel will go out, and make fires with the weapons and burn them, both shields and bucklers, bows and arrows, war clubs and spears and for seven years they will make fires of them. And they will not take wood from the field or gather firewood from the forests, for they will make the

51

spoil of those who despoiled them, and seize the plunder of those who plundered them, declares the Lord God. And it will come about on that day that I shall give Gog a burial ground there in Israel, the valley of those who pass by east of the sea, and it will block off the passer-by. So they will bury Gog there with all his multitudes, and they will call it the valley of Hamon-gog. For seven months the house of Israel will be burying them in order to cleanse the land.'" (Ezekiel 38:18 thru 39:12)

Well, now you know more about the next prophetic battle than do the military leaders who now train for it. It could be that close!

Writers, scholars, and students of the Bible do not claim to know for sure whether or not the "torrential rain, with hailstones, fire, and brimstone," are sent directly from heaven (literally), or if they describe a nuclear exchange. What they do agree upon, as I do, is that it doesn't much matter. It's going to be disastrous any way you look at it.

The Antichrist's forces protecting Israel will certainly have nuclear capabilities. Remember, he heads up the ten-nation European Union (revived Roman Empire) whose member nations are known to have nuclear weapons. It is very difficult to know where the United States fits into this prophecy since most prophecy centers on the Middle East, "the center of the world". But there is one likely place the U.S. may be referenced.

In Ezekiel 39:6, from the passage just quoted, we read: "And I shall send fire upon Magog *and those who inhabit the coastlands in safety*; and they will know that I am the Lord."

The Hebrew word that was translated "coastlands" is *ai,* and usually referred to other continents of gentile civilizations. This surely broadens the scope of the Lord's response to this attack on Israel. Every continent could be included in this battle, either directly by sending troops, or indirectly by supporting it or remaining neutral and doing nothing. I cannot conceive that the U.S. would be directly involved but could perhaps be weary of involvement and be standing on the sidelines either restrained or so weak from other problems it cannot help. There are any number of scenarios I'm sure every reader could visualize. But it's all speculation as to what the role of the U.S. will be in this horrible war - a war that's part of the judgments in Revelation that describe the last seven years of great human suffering and environmental disasters.

ISRAEL AFTER THE DUST SETTLES

The passage in Ezekiel says that Israel will be burying the dead to cleanse the land for seven months (Ezekiel 39:12). And they will be making fires with the weapons for seven years (Ezekiel 39:9). This will bring them into the Millennium still burning these weapons, since there is less than seven years remaining in the Tribulation and Christ's physical return to earth. Remember, this attack begins when Israel is resting in "safety", deceived into thinking they were protected by the seven-year peace treaty that the EU leader (Antichrist) helped broker. This seven-year period is the last remaining period before Christ's visible return with His saints to establish His Kingdom on earth.

At this point, you may be asking, "Why all this destruction?"

If we keep in mind that God's only purpose in allowing such physical destruction is to bring about spiritual repentance, then we can at least see the only positive lining in these events.

How badly hurt is Israel from this war? She clearly had divine intervention come to her rescue. But what were her losses? There is no specific word given on exactly what her losses might have been.

Zechariah does record a death toll in Israel as two-thirds of the population, with one-third coming "through the fire." Whether it's this major war or the overall impact of the Antichrist's campaign against the Jews in the last part of the seven-year period, we can't be sure. Nevertheless, one-third of the nation will come through a refining process to a point where they repent and "call on My name." And again, this is God's ultimate purpose.

"And it will come about in all the land,' declares the Lord, 'that two parts in it will be cut off and perish; but the third will be left in it. And I will bring the third part through the fire, refine them as silver is refined, and test them as gold is tested; they will call on My name, and I will answer them; I will say, "They are My people," and they will say, "The Lord is My God.'"

(Zechariah 13:8,9)

THE ANTICHRIST'S FINAL PREPARATION

After the defeat of the northern alliance that dared attack Israel, the Antichrist takes advantage of the times. As already discussed in previous chapters, He enters the Jews' Temple, declares himself God, and demands the world's worship. He persecutes every Jew he can find, as well as every Christian, since they are trying to expose him for who he really is, Satan in the flesh! Terrible judgments have fallen on "continents" as well as on Israel.

Then, towards the end of the Tribulation, in the closing moments of this seven-year period, forces are converging again on Israel from the east and the north. The battle of Armageddon is shaping up.

The eastern armies are coming as described in Revelation 16:12. They are headed up by China, the only nation in the region interested in being a world power and exercising her muscle. For some reason they are motivated to start their march across land to Israel, where the Antichrist has set himself up to be worshipped as God. Israel's defeat of Russia has already made its mark on the landscape of world events. But it was not the Armageddon, that final battle of all nations against Israel. That will occur a few years later.

Chapter 7

Jerusalem's Temple Reconstructed

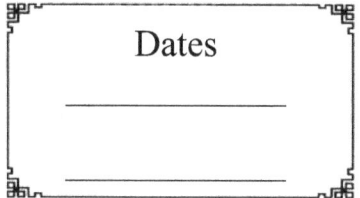

Dates

_____

_____

"And forces from him will arise, desecrate the sanctuary fortress, and do away with the regular sacrifice. And they will set up the abomination of desolation." (Daniel 11:31)

"And he will make a firm covenant with the many for one week, but in the middle of the week he will put a stop to sacrifice and grain offering; and on the wing of abominations will come one who makes desolate..." (Daniel 9:27)

These verses make astounding predictions! The new world leader, spoken of in the previous chapter and identified as the Antichrist, makes a seven-year agreement with the Jews. And right in the middle of it he breaks his word and ends their practices of worship, enters their temple, and boldly proclaims himself to be God. But what we want to focus on here is the fact that for him to be able to do this, there must be a temple. The Jews have had only two temples throughout their 4000 years of history, and at present they have none. So, for the Antichrist to enter this temple, *it will first have to be built.*

Israel (Judaism) has not been able to practice temple worship since their last temple was destroyed by the Romans in 70 AD. *There has been no temple since then.* Occupying nations have not allowed another to be built. In fact, the Mohammedan (Arab) Empire eventually built the Mosque of Omar (Dome of the Rock) on the old temple site in Jerusalem. This is the hilltop King David bought, on which Solomon, his son, would build the first temple around 1,000 BC.

Solomon's temple (the first temple) was destroyed by the Babylonian king Nebuchadnezzar in 587 BC. The second temple was rebuilt by returning exiles coming from Babylon from 537 BC to 515 BC, under the leadership of Zerubbabel.[1] This second temple deteriorated and was eventually refurbished by King Herod between 20 BC and 64 AD. This was the temple Jesus of Nazareth came to and predicted would also be destroyed:

> "And He answered and said to them, `Do you not see all these things? Truly I say to you, not one stone here shall be left upon another, which will not be torn down." (Matthew 24:2)

57

In 70 AD the Romans did just that. And the Jews were scattered throughout the world in what has been called the "diaspora"- the dispersion.

THE TWO TEMPLES

Such a rich history surrounds these temples, I want to share some of the highlights so that you will appreciate how significant the third temple will be when it is built.

The first temple was constructed by Solomon, Israel's third king, in 959 BC. It took seven and a half years to build. God gave the dimensions to David, which were used by his son, Solomon, to build it. David had been storing up materials for it during his reign: 120 million ounces of gold; 1.2 billion ounces of silver; and unknown amounts of bronze and Lebanese cedar. It was 90 feet long, 30 feet wide, and 45 feet high, with a courtyard of 300 feet by 600 feet. And as Dr. H.L Willmington documents for us in his book The King Is Coming, "It was built of blocks of stone quarried in the nearby hills. The inside was paneled with finely carved cedar wood overlaid with gold...All this was done without the sound of hammer, axe, or any other tool (1 Kings 6:7)."[2] This temple lasted for 373 years as it was destroyed by Nebuchadnezzar in 586 BC as the Israelites were taken captive into Babylon.

The second temple was constructed by returning Israelites exiled in Babylon for 70 years. Construction was started by Zerubbabel in 535 BC and completed 19 years later in 516 BC. Herod the Great, the Roman King ruling over Jerusalem in 20 BC, reconstructed and added to this temple until its completion in 64 AD. This was the temple Jesus taught in during His earthly life. "It was the most beautiful building in the world. Herod had trained 1000 priests in building arts and had employed 10,000 skilled masons...The temple was made of beautiful marble and gold so gleaming that it appeared from afar as a mountain of snow glittering in the sun. It could easily hold 120,000 worshipers."[3]

This was the temple where the disciples worshipped with Christ. It was the temple that Jesus Christ was dedicated as a baby in (Luke 2:27); asked questions in (Luke 2:46); taught in (John 7:14); healed in(Matthew 21:14); turned over the tables of the money changers in (John 2: 14,15); predicted its destruction (Matthew 23:37-24:2); and had its veil supernaturally torn in two at His death (Matthew 27:51).

THE NEXT TEMPLE

The next temple will be the third one in Israel's history. The Jews in Israel are now planning the design, the construction, the furnishings, and the operations of the new temple. One organization, The Temple Institute, located in the Old City of Jerusalem, is dedicated to just that.

The institute was founded in 1987 by Rabbi Yisrael Ariel and is a non-profit educational and religious organization with a declared mission "to rekindle the flame of the Holy Temple in the hearts of mankind…and to do as much as possible to bring about the building of the Holy Temple in our time"[4]

One of the things they do is declare the facts not generally known to the public: "Do you realize that Jerusalem was never the capital of any people in the world, other than the Jewish people? And never an Arab capital? The same word 'Jerusalem' which appears in the Bible over 700 times, does not appear in the Koran even once. And yet today, the Higher Islamic Commission of Jerusalem declared that 'there will be no peace or stability in the region or the world without the return of occupied Jerusalem as an Arab and Islamic capital of the sacred Palestinian state.' Their declaration stated that Christian occupation of Christian holy places in Jerusalem must end as well."[5]

The Institute is also making "great strides forward in Temple development, research, awareness, and physical preparation. In the past year, the Temple Institute has reached an important milestone: "We have completed the three most central vessels for Temple service. The golden Menorah, the Incense Altar, and the Table of the Showbread have been completed in all their glory and magnificence, and these vessels are now ready to take their place in the soon-to-be-built Holy Temple."[6]

One of the mysteries surrounding this prophecy of the third temple is the exact location. Where will it be built? Most all scholars agree it has to be built on the same site as the previous two, Mount

Moriah, the place where Abraham offered up Isaac (Genesis 22:2), the hilltop King David bought. But this site once covered 22 acres, but has grown to 35 acres, and is occupied by uncovered walls and partial ruins from the previous two temples as well as Islamic shrines and mosques. So there is a real serious conflict on where and how a Jewish temple can be built on the same site. A brief history of some of the events that have made their imprint on this site will shed more light on our understanding it today.

This is the same site of the first and second temple. It is the same site where when Jerusalem fell to Islam in 639 AD, the Moslem shrine, the Dome of the Rock, was built and completed in 691 AD.[7] This shrine is the third holiest in the Moslem world, an octagonal building that proports to cover the rock that bears the footprints of their prophet Mohammad as he arose to immortality.[8] This site was the focus of rejoicing for the Israeli army when they captured it from Arab control during the six-day war in June of 1967. From Israel's rebirth as a nation in 1948, up to 1967, no Jew was allowed to come near the wall on this site. But on June 7, 1967, Uzi Narkiss, Major General and Central Commander of the Israeli paratroopers, was given the order to take Jerusalem. The next week, June 14, 200,000 Jews went to the wall to celebrate one of their religious feasts. Immediately, Time Magazine was publishing an article, "Should the Temple Be rebuilt?". And the mood of all Israel during these past 55 years since the 1967 take-over of Jerusalem is best summed up by one of the rabbi's remarks during the dedication of the main Jewish

Synagogue in the Jewish section of Jerusalem: "As the city has been reunited in our lifetime, so will the temple be accomplished in our lifetime."[9]

As you can see, the Temple is a major factor in all that entangles the complex struggle for the rule and possession of Jerusalem. The Temple, the Temple! Where will it be built? How can it be built when the Dome of the Rock sits on what many believe to be the exact site of the other temples? These persisting and gnawing questions fill the air.

As we consider all the talk and plans of where and how this next Temple might be built, I want to strongly suggest we don't narrow the possibilities to only one event, i.e., the destruction of the Dome of the Rock and the subsequent rebuilding of the Temple. There have been attempts by religious radicals to bomb the shrine just for this purpose. But recent archaeological finds have shown the original footprint of the previous temples, although nearby on the mount, may not have been the exact same location as the existing shrine. That is what one prominent archaeologist has declared after years of research.

Dr. Kaufman, an archaeologist who has spent 16 years investigating the Temple Mount, published his findings in March 1983 in the *Biblical Archaeology Review*. As Hal Lindsey states in There's a New World Coming, "Although all of the extensive evidence upon which Dr. Kaufman bases his establishment of the

Temple foundation's exact location cannot be given here, I am convinced after carefully checking his evidence personally on the Temple Mount that he is absolutely correct. The most obvious evidence that the golden Dome of the Rock could not be over the Temple site is its proximity to the Eastern Gate. Every ancient document describing the Temple placed the Eastern gate exactly on the east/west centerline of the Temple itself. The Dome of the Rock is at least 150 meters south of that centerline. A little domed cupola sitting inconspicuously on the northwest corner of the present Temple platform ...is called the 'Dome of the Tablets' and also the 'Dome of the Spirits.' It covers one of the only two exposed protrusions of bedrock in the ancient Temple area. This little piece of bedrock is exactly on the east/west centerline of the ancient Eastern gate."[10]

There is also another possibility that is talked about. It proposes that the "Jerusalem Great Synagogue", built in 1982 "as a central, representative sanctuary to which pilgrims from all over the world may come to pray – just as they did in the Temple of old",[11] will be converted into a Temple when the time comes. It may not satisfy the purists because of its location. It may not even satisfy God Himself, but this will certainly not deter the fraudulent Antichrist from entering the Temple. He plans to desecrate it anyway. And this Temple will probably suffer great damage and be destroyed during the great earthquakes of the last three-and-one-half years after the Antichrist breaks his treaty.

ARK OF THE COVENANT

One of the most central pieces of furniture that needs to be placed in the new Temple once it is fully operational, is the Ark of the Covenant. This is one piece even the Temple Institute cannot, and dare not try to, duplicate because of its holy and historical significance. According to the biblical accounts and Jewish history, it was constructed in a certain way as described in Exodus, chapter 25. Made out of acacia wood, it was a chest that housed three irreplaceable things: a gold jar of manna, Aaron's staff that had budded, and the two tablets on which were inscribed the Ten Commandments as the basic stipulations of the Sinai covenant when Moses received the law on Mount Sinai (See Hebrews 9). The chest had a cover called the Mercy Seat made out of pure gold with an angel called a cherub at both ends with open wings. The cover was to be made of one solid piece, including the cherubim. And the presence of God was to come between the two cherubim on this Mercy Seat.

So how do you recreate or replace such a holy thing as the Ark of the Covenant with its precious contents? *You don't. You just set out to find it.* Hence the movie industry's version of the "Raiders of the Lost Ark". But unlike any fiction movie, reality is even more exciting. Many theories abound as to what happened to the Ark, and as to where it is located.

Here is what the Temple Institute tells us: "Tradition records that even as King Solomon built the First Temple, he already knew, through divine inspiration, that eventually it would be destroyed. Thus Solomon, the wisest of all men, oversaw the construction of a vast system of labyrinths, mazes, chambers, and corridors underneath the Temple Mount complex."

They also explain how this fact infuriates the Arab population as excavations by archeologists continue to search for the lost Ark near the Temple Mount: "They stand a great deal to lose if the Ark is revealed -- for it will prove to the whole world that there really was a Holy Temple, and thus, that the Jews really do have a claim to the temple Mount. (The official position of the Islamic Wakf, the body that governs over the Temple Mount, is that there never was a Holy Temple. And that the Jews have no rights whatsoever to the place)."[12]

So once again, we have men trying to discover exactly where, and controlling when, the Temple will be built. We have radicals trying to blow up buildings, and rabbis preparing plans. The Temple Institute, is dedicated to the research and preparation of the furniture, instruments, and priests to be used in the new Temple. Nonetheless, God is in control, and He will guide events towards the *right location at the right time. **And you will recognize and record the date**.* You will see the materials assembled and prepared for erection. You will see the peace treaty signed allowing the Jews to build their Temple. You will see the ceremonies dedicating the Temple and the

Jews worshiping for the first time since 70 AD. You will see the Antichrist walk into the temple three-and-one-half years later (after the signing of the peace treaty) and declare himself a god.

You do not have to take my word or anyone else's at this point. If you're a gambler and want to risk waiting until you "see it with your own eyes", then wait. Perhaps when you finally do see these events, you will at least acknowledge that they had been prophesied for thousands of years. Mark the date when it occurs. And be ready for other events.

Chapter 8

The Resurrection and Rapture

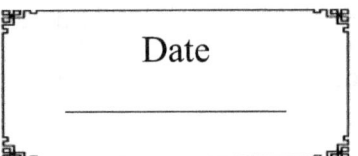

Date

_____

"Behold, I tell you a mystery; we shall not all sleep, but we shall all be changed, in a moment, in the twinkling of an eye, at the last trumpet; for the trumpet will sound, and the dead will be raised imperishable, and we shall be changed."

(1 Corinthians 15:51, 52)

"For the Lord Himself will descend from heaven with a shout, with the voice of the archangel, and with the trumpet of God; and the dead in Christ shall rise first. Then we who are alive and remain shall be caught up together with them in the clouds to meet the Lord in the air, and thus we shall always be with the Lord."

(1 Thessalonians 4:16, 17)

"And just as it happened in the days of Noah, so it will be also in the days of the Son of Man. They were eating, they were drinking, they were marrying, they were being given in marriage, until the day that Noah entered the ark, and the flood came and destroyed them all." "I tell you, on that night there will be two in bed; one will be taken and the other will be left."   (Luke 17: 26-27; 34-35)

This Resurrection-Rapture event is the enormously anticipated "gathering" of His believers, ever since the beginning of time to the day it happens. The Church is watching all the signs and events so as to track the approach of this *one* event.

For a couple of centuries, the Church has been referring to this coming event as the "rapture". This is a good description of the event since those believers who are still alive will be "snatched up" or "gathered together" just as Jesus was when He left this earth, in visible fashion, before hundreds of witnesses into the clouds. But we must not overlook the fact that the great biblical event called the "Resurrection" is part of this Rapture, as the verses above so clearly state. Our bodies being resurrected and joined with our spirit is precisely what believers have hoped and longed for these last six thousand years. And you can find it referenced hundreds of times in the Scriptures, both the Old and New Testaments.

This chapter discusses the first phase of Jesus' second coming, His second advent. His first advent covered 33 years as He walked the earth as our Savior. But now, His second coming, as you will see, involves some amazing events as He now shows up as King and Lord, beginning with the resurrection and the rapture of His believers. This chapter could just as well have been called "The Second Coming of Jesus Christ, Phase 1." But since the resurrection and rapture give a greater description of His actions and our blessing during this initial appearance, I named it as such.

With that in mind, allow me to explain why I entitled Chapter 15 "The Second Coming of Jesus Christ." In that chapter I describe the next events we see and read about in Revelation as Jesus takes His church to heaven for the Judgment Seat of Christ (believers receive just rewards), and the marriage of the Lamb (believers are wedded to Christ), and finally the return to earth (Phase 2) with His bride, saints in white linen clothing, to the earth to help fight in the battle of Armageddon and bring an end to the destruction of mankind.

Now to the subject of this initial, first phase of His second coming and appearance as He comes to resurrect his believers.

THE RESURRECTIONS

There are two kinds of resurrections planned "for all who are in the tombs".

> "Do not marvel at this; for an hour is coming, in which all who are in the tombs shall hear His voice and shall come forth; those who did the good deeds, to a resurrection of life, those who committed the evil deeds to a resurrection of judgment." (John 5:28, 29)

69

It's important to realize that after this life, and after the physical death, comes a resurrection for everyone! Now that might be news to many, nevertheless that's what we're told here. But the real message is how the two groups are treated; one resurrected to life, and the other to judgment and a *second death*. See what these other scriptures say about this second death.

"He who has an ear, let him hear what the Spirit says to the churches. He who overcomes shall not be hurt by the second death." (Revelation 2:11)

"He who overcomes shall inherit these things, and I will be his God and he will be My son. But for the cowardly and unbelieving and abominable and murderers and immoral persons and sorcerers and idolaters and all liars, their part will be in the lake that burns with fire and brimstone, which is the second death." (Revelation 21:7-8)

We are instructed numerous times in the scriptures on how to be worthy enough to be part of the first resurrection, to eternal life. But there is one verse that makes it crystal clear:

"He who believes in the Son has eternal life; but he who does not obey the Son shall not see life, but the wrath of God abides on him." (John 3:36)

70

Those who have died with Christ as their Savior and Lord, will be a part of this first resurrection. There will be no second death for them.

> "...and they came to life and reigned with Christ for a thousand years. The rest of the dead did not come to life until the thousand years were completed. This is the first resurrection. Blessed and holy is the one who has a part in the first resurrection; over these the second death has no power..."
>
> (Revelation 20:4-6)

The first resurrection is set aside for followers of Christ. The second resurrection will take place 1,000 years later, after the Millennium, and is reserved for all those who don't follow Christ (the unbelievers). Following this second resurrection is a second death.

"And I saw a great white throne and Him who sat upon it, from whose presence earth and heaven fled away, and no place was found for them. And I saw the dead, the great and the small, standing before the throne, and books were opened; and another book was opened, which is the book of life; and the dead were judged from the things which were written in the books. According to their deeds. And the sea gave up the dead which were in it, and death and Hades gave up the dead which were in them; and they were judged, every one of them according to their deeds. And death and Hades were thrown into the lake of fire. This is the second death, the lake of fire. And if anyone's name was not found written in the book of life, he was thrown into the lake of fire."   (Revelation 20:11-15)

A multitude of people wish these verses were not in this great book. It makes their destiny all too clear. And did you notice how there were many books opened for those who will experience the second death, but only one book of life? Sadly enough, the majority of mankind has chosen to live ungodly, selfish lives rather than a clean, godly one. Only one book records the names of these faithful. Will your name be written there?

It's important to point out something about the first resurrection. I personally believe it will include all those Old Testament faithful (who looked forward to Christ), the New Testament faithful called "Christians" (who look back towards Christ), and all those living when the Resurrection and Rapture occur. Some scholars do not agree and tell us the Old Testament believers will appear in heaven at a later time. But they have no convincing biblical evidence to support this.

If you're able to record the date of this major event, the Resurrection and gathering up of those yet alive (Rapture), *then you have missed the main event!*

Millions of religious people will find themselves in this same situation - *left behind*. The apostasy referenced earlier will blind many millions from the truth. But because of their apostasy and weak or non-existent faith, they will not be strong enough to reject Antichrist's new monetary system and accompanying mark (See Chapter 9, Mark of the Beast). They were not strong enough, faithful enough, committed enough, willing enough to face starvation, persecution, and death by execution by the Antichrist's administration. In short, they were not able to become one of those martyrs spoken of in Revelation 20:4.

TIMING OF RESURRECTION AND RAPTURE

This brings us to another critical issue regarding this Resurrection and Rapture. When will it occur so that we can be ready for it? Bible scholars have differed on the timing of the Rapture as either happening *before* the Tribulation (pre-tribulation), *during* the Tribulation (mid-tribulation), or *after* the Tribulation during the last few weeks or hours of the Tribulation (post-tribulation). (See Chapter 3, Seven Years of Trouble.)

Let's be clear, since this is an issue that does not affect a person's faith in Christ as Savior and Lord, it is not a matter of your salvation or eternal life hinging on you being right or wrong on this issue of the "timing" of the Rapture. The all-important issue for salvation and eternal life is a personal relationship with Christ. He is willing to overlook one's error in defending or believing what may be the wrong timing. All respectable Bible scholars and ministers agree on this.

I point this out so that new believers and newcomers to Bible prophecy will learn to be tolerant with others who may have differing opinions on issues such as this. This attitude has helped me personally always to be open to new truth and revelation as God leads.

So, when do I believe the Rapture will happen? I believe there is overwhelming evidence that places it *around the middle of* the Tribulation, a mid-tribulation position. Since there is not one single verse that says clearly the Resurrection and Rapture will come in the middle of, or before, the Tribulation, it is important to study and divide the word of God carefully in order to come to your own best conclusion.

Every preacher, evangelist, missionary, and Christian author expounds on their position as to when the Rapture will occur. (They seldom use the term Resurrection, although we should all know this means that both occur at the same time). I've always respected a variety of views, learning something from each of them as well as my own observations. That is why I want to summarize the key points used to argue the two most widely held positions on the timing of the Rapture.

PRE-TRIBULATION RATIONALE

Here are some of the strong reasons that contribute to the understanding that Christ will "gather up" (resurrect; rapture) His church *before* the seven-year Tribulation and the final war, Armageddon.

1) <u>The Resurrection and Rapture</u> will happen one day, but we do not "know the day or the hour" (Matthew 24: 36). But we can know the **season** by watching the signs in order not to be unprepared. (Luke 21:3,4; Mark 32:32-37)

2) <u>God has not destined believers to wrath.</u> (1 Thessalonians.1:10; and 5:9) Therefore believers will experience the Rapture **before** God's wrath is poured out.

3) <u>Believers spend time in their Father's house.</u> (John 14:1-3) **After** believers are resurrected and raptured, they experience the Marriage Supper with their Lord (Revelation 19:7) (bride and bridegroom). And they receive their rewards, at the Judgment Seat of Christ. according to the materials sent up during their lifetime, their good deeds on earth. (2 Corinthians 5:10; and 3:12-15)

4) <u>The Lord's return will be like a thief in the night.</u> (1 Thessalonians 5:1-4) And we shall all be changed in the blink of an eye. (1 Corinthians 15:51-52). Those holding to

75

this position believe this will occur so fast that only the chaos left behind because of the missing will demonstrate something strange has occurred. (See the mid-tribulation rationale on this event to see a stark contrast from a "secret" Rapture, to a very visible one!)

Note: Both positions hold these <u>same four beliefs</u> mentioned above as their foundation to why, when, and how the Rapture will occur. But as both positions study and identify other events that give reference to sequencing and timing, you will see how they diverge and come to their different conclusions.

5) <u>The Rapture event is imminent and will occur before the Tribulation period (7 years)</u>. It could surprise us **any day** meaning no other biblical events are required or expected before this surprise event. (Because John was "called up" in Revelation 4:1 to see the revelation of all that was to come on this earth during the last days, it is symbolic that the Rapture is also a "calling up.")

6) <u>The Holy Spirit is the restrainer</u>. He is holding back the revealing of the Antichrist and his plan to rule a new world order. Only when the believers, as salt and light of the world (Church), are removed through the Rapture, does it allow the lawless one to begin his goal of ruling the new world during the Tribulation period. Thus, we have the pre-tribulation position.

"And you know what restrains him now, so that in his time he will be revealed. For the mystery of lawlessness is already at work: only he who now restrains him will do so until he is taken out of the way. Then the lawless one will be revealed whom the Lord will slay with the breath of His mouth and bring to an end by the appearance of His coming." (2 Thessalonians 2:6-8)

7) The Church is not mentioned any time after Revelation 4:1. This supposedly means that since the word "church" is not found during any of the events from Revelation 4-19, it is because it **has been raptured**. (No valid reasoning is given as to why the mention of "saints" throughout many of these same chapters would not indicate that the Church was **still here**).

MID-TRIBULATION RATIONALE

1) The Resurrection and Rapture. (Same as Pre-Tribulation view)

2) God has not destined believers to wrath. (Same as Pre-Tribulation view)

3) Believers spend time in their Father's house. (Same as Pre-Tribulation view)

4) The Lord's return will be like a thief in the night. (Same as

Pre-Tribulation view)

The Mid-Tribulation position does also believe the change that takes place in the believer, in a twinkling of an eye, and is the transformation from the mortal form to the immortal form, as Jesus demonstrated Himself. Yes, they believe it is instantaneous. But that does not necessarily mean the entire event is unseen by the world, but rather is visible as Matthew 24: 27 says: "for as the lightening comes from the east and flashes to the west, so also will be the coming of the Son of Man be." The change is instantaneous, but the entire event is seen by the world.

5) <u>Timing of the Rapture is "at that time."</u> Before God's wrath is poured out, before the seventh seal is opened, the Rapture occurs. In the gospel of Mathew 24: 29-31, and years later when John is writing Revelation 6:12-13, both describe the same event as <u>the sun turns black, the moon becomes like blood, and the stars of the sky fall to earth.</u> The context of each of them helps place a timing of the Rapture.

In Matthew, Jesus is answering the question in verse 24:3: "...what will be the sign of Your coming and of the end of the age?" And among the many signs, one of which was the "Abomination of Desolation" (the Antichrist stepping into the Temple's Holy of Holies and declaring that he is God) he ends his warning with these three signs and then says: "THEN (in other versions, "at this time") the sign of the Son of Man will appear in the sky, and then all the tribes of the earth will mourn, and they will see the Son of Man coming on the clouds of the sky with power and great glory. And He will send forth His angels with a great trumpet, and they will <u>gather together</u> His elect from the four winds, from one end of the sky to the other." (Matthew 24:30, 31)

This "gathering together" is the Rapture phase of Jesus' Second Coming. Even though the day and hour are not known, we are being given events to watch for. And when you see these SAME signs mentioned in Revelation 6:12, 13, we can now place its timing before the seventh seal which introduces the seven angels with seven trumpets which are well into the seven years of Tribulation.

6) <u>Rapture will not occur until at least six other major events are seen.</u> Two scriptures point clearly to more timing clues:

"Now we request you, brethren, with regard to the coming of our Lord Jesus Christ and our gathering together to Him, that you not be quickly shaken from your composure or be disturbed either by a spirit or message or letter as from us, to the effect that the Day of the Lord has come. Let no one in any way deceive you, for it will not come unless the apostasy comes first, and the man of lawlessness is revealed, the son of destruction, who opposes and exalts himself above every so-called god or object of worship, so that he takes his seat in the temple of God, displaying himself as being God."

(1 Thessalonians 2: 1-4)

"Therefore, when you see the Abomination of Desolation which was spoken of by Daniel the prophet, standing in the Holy place, …for then there will be great tribulation such as has not occurred since the beginning of the world until now, nor ever will."   (Matthew 24: 15, 21)

Both of these scriptures warn believers to watch for the Abomination of Desolation. It is a milestone event that tells us much about the timing of the Rapture because this event is precisely in the middle of the seven-year treaty, the middle of the Tribulation. And since there are many other circumstances that must happen prior to seeing this Antichrist step into the Temple, we can logically conclude as John Shorey has in his book *The Window of the Lord's Return* that five other events have also occurred: 1) A One World Government has been established; 2) The Great Falling Away has occurred; 3) The Antichrist has been revealed; 4) The Temple has been Built; 5) Specific Heavenly Events have occurred

80

(sun turns black, moon turns blood red; stars fall from sky).

7) <u>The Restrainer is the Archangel Michael not the Holy Spirit</u>.

It is very convenient for the pre-tribulation position to conclude that since the Rapture will occur before all seven years of the Tribulation, and since the Holy Spirit lives within the Church, that it most probably is the Holy Spirit who is restraining the lawless one from being revealed. The Church is raptured, the Holy Spirit is gone, and now the Antichrist can be revealed. Sounds very logical. And they give some very convincing scriptural reasons.

But I prefer to consider strongly John Shorey's careful explanation that it is Michael the archangel that has been restraining the Antichrist until which time the Lord commands him to "stand down." He points out that Michael has the power to restrain evil:

"Now at that time Michael, the great prince who stands guard over the sons of your people, will arise. And there will be a time of distress such as never occurred since there was a nation until that time; and at that time your people, everyone who is found written in the book, will be rescued." (Daniel 12:1)

As you can see, Michael clearly has the power to restrain evil. And Shorey concludes by pointing out: "Now if Michael, one of God's generals who commands the armies of God can protect us from evil forces, then does it not make sense that if God wants to allow the forces of evil to rise up on the earth in the person of the Antichrist, that God could tell Michael, one of his top generals, to stand down." [1]

In many biblical occasions, Michael the archangel is seen fighting and restraining evil. Just one of them is when there was war in heaven when Michael fought the devil and his angels, only for them to be thrown down to the earth (Revelation 12: 7-10).

Since the Lord will decide when to reveal the Antichrist, and when he will make the seven-year treaty (Tribulation begins), we now can understand how the Church is still on earth, Holy Spirit included, as the Tribulation commences.

8) <u>Saints are martyred.</u> During the first half of the Tribulation, the Antichrist is "waging war with the saints and overpowering them" (Daniel 7: 21). Clearly the Church, the saints, have not been raptured. The apostate church, the false prophet, and the Antichrist's decree to take his mark in order to buy or sell anything is taking a toll on believers. This is the most important reason to not put your 100% belief in the pre-tribulation position. Because if you are expecting to be

removed before all of this persecution hits because you believed you would be raptured, it is very likely you could be disillusioned, weakened in your faith, and submit to the Antichrist's requirements to take his mark in order to survive. We cannot allow that to happen. As the next chapter, Chapter 9: The Mark of the Beast, will detail, the saints need to be strong in their faith and committed to the Lord as the Antichrist tries to force them to take the mark or be killed (Rev. 14:9-13). Believers will need to die for their faith as millions of others have done down through the ages. The Resurrection and Rapture are just around the corner.

9) Wrath of God doesn't begin until seventh seal. Think of it this way: the first seven seals are not announced by angels and are not written inside the scroll. The wrath of God is delivered by angels and is written inside the scroll. The first seven seals appear to be more of the devil's wrath than from God.

The sixth seal is the same sign as Jesus described in Matthew 24:29 (No. 5 above) as he describes things we are to watch for: the sun darkened, the moon will not give its light, and the stars will fall from the sky. Believers are still here, watching, and yes suffering from persecution. But the wrath of God has not yet begun until you see what is written right before the seventh seal:

"And they said to the mountains and to the rocks, 'Fall on us and hide us from the presence of Him who sits on the throne, and from the wrath of the Lamb; for the great day of their wrath has come, and who is able to stand.'" (Revelation 6:16, 17)

Then a few verses later we learn that there are four angels waiting to harm the earth and the sea but are told by another angel not to do so until the 144,000 Jews are anointed with the seal of God.

"Do not harm the earth or the sea or the trees until we have sealed the bond-servants of our God on their foreheads." (Revelation 7:3)

All of this is leading up to the seventh seal which is really the introduction of seven angels with seven trumpets which BEGIN THE WRATH OF GOD.

"When the Lamb broke the seventh seal, there was silence in heaven for about half an hour. And I saw the seven angels who stand before God, and seven trumpets were given to them." (Revelation 8:1,2)

BOTH POSITIONS HAVE MERIT

I have done my best to summarize the two most widely held views of the timing of the Resurrection-Rapture covering the main points. Each position has many other points to support their view as they try to connect all the doctrines and timing issues to support their view. And even though I showed my preference for the Mid-Tribulation position, I believe it is my responsibility to ask you to be watching for both possibilities to develop. **That is why I have emphasized the date-setting potential we all have before us**.

The truth remains, that no one knows how long their life will be and must prepare spiritually now. Yes, we should be living our life looking to: the imminent day of our natural death and the imminent Resurrection-Rapture no matter which doctrinal position is correct.

Note: The post-tribulation position has not been discussed here since most scholars do not believe it is plausible and is not supported by, and is in violation of, much of scripture.

Chapter 9

Mark of The Beast

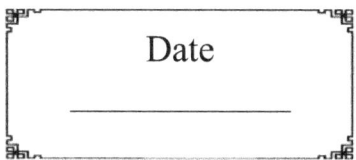

Date

_____

"...And he causes all, the small and the great, and the rich and the poor, and the free men and the slaves to be given a mark on their right hand or on their forehead. And he provides that no one should be able to buy or to sell, except the one who has the mark, either the name of the beast or the number of his name."

(Revelation 13:16, 17)

It wasn't so clear years ago how something like this could ever happen. But today's technology leaves nothing to the imagination. Electronic Funds Transfer (EFT) is allowing the banking system to centralize and to eventually eliminate the need for money. Experiments conducted thirty years ago when my first book, *Apocalypse Soon*, was first started, have now developed into widespread use throughout the world. And whereas credit cards are used nowadays, the next step is to protect the consumer from theft and have all his medical information immediately available by placing his account number on his hand or head. This technology is also already being developed. And since September 11, 2001, there is a serious need for secure identification that cannot be faked. Enter the modern-day inventors.

Just as I was compelled to write this book when 9-11 occurred, a New Jersey surgeon, in cooperation with Applied Digital Solutions of Palm Beach, was compelled to inject microchips into his left forearm and right leg as an experiment to develop a secure form of identification. David Streitfeld of the *Times* Staff writes in the December 19, 2001 issue of the *Los Angeles Times* (A Chip ID That's Only Skin-Deep), "'There's no deformity of the skin', Seelig said. "'I feel just the same as I did before.'"

Streitfeld begins his report by saying, "A Florida company is poised to become the first to sell microchips designed to be implanted into human beings, an achievement that opens the door to new systems of medical monitoring and ID screening." He explains how the original purpose of Applied Digital's technology was to assist patients brought into a hospital emergency room unconscious to identify their medical status by way of data on a microchip. Technicians could scan the microchip and learn of any artificial organs or limbs, and diseases or allergic reactions the patient may have.

But there are other more potent applications that could give it a role as the ultimate ID. Streitfeld writes, "'I'd be shocked if within

87

10 years you couldn't get a chip implanted that would unlock your house, start your car and give you money,' says Chris Hables Gray, an associate professor of computer science at the University of Great falls in Montana and author of *The Cyborg Citizen*.

English cyberneticist Kevin Warwick won considerable notoriety over 20 years ago by implanting an electronic transmitter above his left elbow. The implant opened doors and switched on lights at his British University of Reading offices."[1]

It won't take long for the "cyberneticists" of this world to perfect these new systems. While simultaneously the new European leader is moving quietly forward, perhaps unwittingly, ready to help this struggling world achieve peace and prosperity his way.

This world leader will gain the confidence of nations, then help them out of the financial mess they will find themselves in. He could also require them to cooperate with a system based on the use of a microchip ID or any other similar high-tech device. Although the system by itself will not be evil, the leader that gains control over it will be. He is called the Antichrist and will be associated with the number "666".

"...Let him who has understanding calculate the number of the beast, for the number is that of a man, and his number is 666."

(Revelation 13:18)

Severe economic conditions will require a world monetary system such as this. It will be even more severe since it falls into the Antichrist's hands. Because of his preoccupation with being a god, he also considers it a duty for the world citizen to worship him and an image that he sets up. Read carefully the warning and commandment given by God about this. It could save your life!

"And another angel, a third one, followed them, saying in a loud voice, 'If anyone worships the beast and his image, and receives a mark on his forehead or upon his hand, he also will drink of the wine of the wrath of God'" ... (Revelation 14:9-12)

There can't be anything clearer than this. *Anyone who receives the mark will be marked for hell.* That deserves repeating. *Anyone who receives the mark will be marked for hell.* Cooperation with this leader and his system is contrary to God's desire and will. This is obviously where God has drawn the line. So many of man's sins are forgivable...but this one is not! And this will be one of the greatest tests for those who call themselves "Christians" or "believers". Their faith will need to be firmly rooted to give them the courage and strength to "*just say no*" to this mark. Buying and selling will be officially prohibited without it. But God says you will "drink of God's wrath" if you take it. What a choice!

But as difficult as it will be for Christians, it will be even more

89

difficult, nearly impossible, for the uninformed to resist this new requirement. For surely everyone will want to cooperate with our new world leader. Taking a chip or mark on the hand or forehead is not asking much. Yet that is why I want to sound the alarm now while there is time to ponder the impact of such a wild and ominous event.

Chapter 10

Alliance Made in Hell

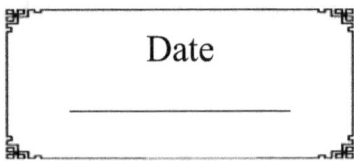
Date
_____

"...And I saw another beast coming up out of the earth; and he had two horns like a lamb, and he spoke as a dragon."

(Revelation 13:11)

H ere comes the wolf in sheep's clothing! The scripture calls him "another beast", since a first beast was described in the beginning ten verses of this chapter 13 of Revelation. The first beast is clearly described as the world leader who is fatally wounded and revived (vs.3). This is the Antichrist, the government leader of the new revived Roman Empire now known as the European Union. (More on his fatal wound in another chapter.)

This other beast is described as a religious leader who makes the earth worship the government leader.

"And he exercises all the authority of the first beast in his presence. And he makes the earth and those who dwell in it to

91

worship the first beast, whose fatal wound was healed."

(Revelation 13:12)

This religious leader also has some unusual powers. Why else would he be so believable?

"And he performs great signs, so that he even makes fire come down out of heaven to the earth in the presence of men."

(Revelation 13:13)

He uses these powers to convince the world that the government leader, the Antichrist, should be worshipped. And those who do not agree are killed.

"And he deceives those who dwell on the earth because of the signs which it was given him to perform in the presence of the beast, telling those who dwell on the earth to make an image to the beast who had the wound of the sword and has come to life. And there was given to him to give breath to the image of the beast, that the image of the beast might even speak and cause as many as do not worship the image of the beast to be killed."

(Revelation 13:14, 15)

Again, we see how clearly the lines will be drawn. You will

need to cooperate with this false prophet (world church leader) and obey his instructions to worship the Antichrist or die.

Many good people are going to be deceived. If they do not know that such a powerful religious leader has been prophesied to do these things, they will easily believe him and accept him as "from God". Only now, you know what's going to happen before it happens. This should strengthen your inner resolve to be ready to stand against these two beasts, even if it costs you your life.

It will be somewhat like the days of Constantine, when he marched into Rome in 312 AD and declared Christianity the official religion. This false prophet will anoint the Antichrist as official leader of the new European Union with extraordinary powers to back it up! And they will demand even greater things as their world leadership grows.

The next chapter will shed more light on how this new one-world religious leader comes to power. Present day events are already pointing to his arrival as the ground is prepared.

Chapter 11

Sin Topples the Church

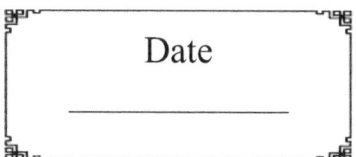

Date
_____

"Let no one in any way deceive you, for it (Second Coming of Jesus Christ) will not come unless the apostasy (falling from the faith) comes first, and the man of lawlessness is revealed, the son of destruction..."   (2 Thessalonians 2:3)

We all know that the "church-goer" is very often criticized by many for his hypocrisy. He is perceived as trying to be holy and good on Sundays but living the same way as everyone else the rest of the week. Unfortunately, this has been a valid judgment by the masses for much of the church's behavior.

Even God Himself is disgusted with this contradiction, but has told the true believers, the genuine church, to allow it, so that He personally may separate the true believers later. Look at this parable that Jesus spoke about just this subject.

> "He presented another parable to them, saying, 'The kingdom of heaven may be compared to a man who sowed good seed in his field. But while men were sleeping, his enemy came and sowed tares (weeds) also among the wheat and went away. But when the wheat sprang up and bore grain, then the tares became evident also. And the slaves of the landowner came and said to him, "Sir, did you not sow good seed in your field? How then does it have tares?" And he said to them, "An enemy has done this!" And the slaves said to him, "Do you want us, then to go and gather them up?" But he said, "No; lest while you are gathering up the tares, you may root up the wheat with them. Allow both to grow together until the time of the harvest; and in the time of the harvest I will say to the reapers, 'First gather up the tares and bind them in bundles to burn them up; but gather the wheat into my barn.'"

> (Matthew 13:24-30)

The day is soon coming when events will test the "church-goer" and his faith. The false cults, false teachings, and deceptions predicted for the end times will dominate the environment as well. You will need to be strong in your faith towards the end. If you are a true believer, you can persevere, even if your own family betrays you. The Bible calls it being an "overcomer."

"But you will be betrayed even by parents and brothers and relatives and friends, and they will put some of you to death, and you will be hated by all on account of My name."

(Luke 21:16,17)

As we approach the last seven-year period called the "Tribulation", we see that religion plays a major role. Religion will be the focal point of the new world leader's (Antichrist) approach to gain world support. He needs a worldwide church to help him unite the revived Roman Empire (Europe).[1]

Look at how biblical prophecy identifies the "fallen away" or apostate church:

"And he carried me away in the Spirit into a wilderness; and I saw a woman sitting on a scarlet beast, full of blasphemous names, having seven heads and ten horns. And the woman was clothed in purple and scarlet, and adorned with gold and precious stones and pearls, having in her hand a gold cup full of abominations and of the unclean things of her immorality, and upon her forehead a name was written, a mystery, "BABYLON THE GREAT, THE MOTHER OF HARLOTS AND OF THE ABOMINATIONS OF THE EARTH." And I saw the woman drunk with the blood of the saints, and with the blood of the witnesses of Jesus. And when I saw her, I wondered greatly." (Revelation 17:3-6)

96

Babylon is used to symbolize this fallen church, called here the "mother of the harlots" because Babylon was known for representing a sad chapter in the history of God's people, the Jews. A period where they mixed their belief with others to gain converts. As a prostitute or harlot would do, they sold out to another false religion that was prevalent in their land. The Tower of Babel (Genesis 11:4) represents the beginning of idol worship, where hand-carved idols were kept in the top room of the tower.[2] This tower was in Babylon, located not far from Bagdad, Iraq.

During this period, one of Noah's grandsons, Nimrod, was using his evil ways to start a new kind of idol worship. He and his wife, Semerimus, knew God had promised a Savior would one day be sent to lead their people. So they decided to claim that their son, Tammuz, was the fulfillment of that prophecy. With this extraordinary claim, Semerimus encouraged that she and her son be exalted, thus starting a mother and son worship system.[3]

When the tower of Babel was destroyed and the people's languages confused (Genesis 11:5-9), this system spread from Babylon to other areas and took on other names. The Egyptians called the two Isis and Horus, while the Greeks named them Aphrodite and Adonis. And most remembered today are the mother and son called Venus and Cupid, originally adored by the Romans.

This mother-child worship was an abomination to the Lord. He says in the scriptures how much this kindled His wrath.

97

"Then He brought me to the entrance of the gate of the Lord's house which was toward the north; and behold, women were sitting there weeping for Tammuz. And He said to me, "Do you see this, son of man? Yet you will see still greater abominations than these."　　　　(Ezekiel 18:14, 15)

"As for you, do not pray for this people, and do not lift up cry or prayer for them, and do not intercede with Me; for I do not hear you. Do you not see what they are doing in the cities of Judah and in the streets of Jerusalem? The children gather wood, and the fathers kindle the fire, and the women knead dough to make cakes for the queen of heaven; and they pour out libations to other gods in order to spite Me."　　　　(Jeremiah 7:16-18)

Women weeping for the child, Tammuz, and people making cakes and praying to the Queen of Heaven, Semerimus, was a serious error that brought judgment. As an ironic twist, God punishes the Jews by allowing them to be brought into captivity in 606 BC into Babylon for 70 years.

This same Babylon-type church, mother of harlots, will again show a dominance and play a major role in helping the "beast". Remember, the beast which the woman is riding represents the new revived Roman Empire. Another verse tells us who this will be when it says "Here is the mind which has wisdom. The seven heads are seven mountains on which the woman sits..." (Revelation 17:9). Rome is known as the city of seven mountains and could very likely be the seat of this harlot church.

We'll need to watch for a large church, or an ecumenical movement of sorts, joining itself to a world leader. This will be the fulfillment of the prophecy "the woman sits on the beast". Traditional biblical truths will be watered down in order to satisfy the masses, as various ecumenical movements will also join this super-church. It's very important to know the whole purpose behind this falling away and rise of a world church. It ushers in a period of persecution for the *true church*. Look what the next few verses say in this same chapter 17 of Revelation:

"These will wage war against the Lamb, and the Lamb will overcome them, because He is Lord of lords and King of kings, and those who are with Him are the called and chosen and faithful." (Revelation 17:14)

The "Lamb" has always represented Christ and His church. When the world leader comes to power and begins requiring the "mark of the beast" to be applied to everyone's hands or foreheads, the faithful will be severely challenged. The true testing of their faith will be in focus. And as this verse tells us, they will have victory. But the apostate church will be guilty of helping the beast persecute the Lamb.

"And I saw the woman drunk with the blood of the saints, and with the blood of the witnesses of Jesus. And when I saw her, I wondered greatly." (Revelation 17:6)

This apostate church eventually falls from its high position of world respect. When the sins have piled so high, God brings judgment on her acts and the Antichrist himself turns on her:

"And the ten horns which you saw, and the beast, these will hate the harlot, and will make her desolate and naked, and will eat her flesh and will burn her up with fire." (Revelation 17:16)

This apostate church thought she was a queen and would never see mourning. So many think they are doing well with all their ceremonies, large cathedrals, expensive robes, and all the rich surroundings that go along with it. Living sensuously will be "in" for this apostate church as well as the rest of the world, until finally Babylon the harlot church falls. I pray you will not fall with her.

Chapter 12

Two Powerful
Miracle Makers

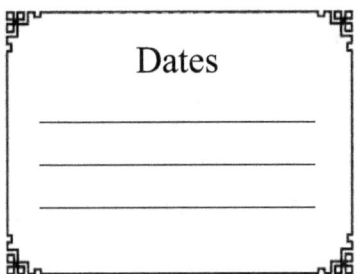

Dates

_____

_____

_____

"And I will grant authority to my two witnesses, and they will prophesy for 1,260 days... and if anyone desires to harm them, fire proceeds out of their mouth and devours their enemies...these have the power to shut up the sky, in order that rain may not fall during the days of their prophesying; and they have power over the waters to turn them into blood, and to smite the earth with every plague, as often as they desire."   (Revelation 11:3-6)

We have already talked about the seven-year period that will occur during the last days when the world leader called Antichrist breaks his agreement after three and a half years, leaving another three and a half years of turmoil for Israel. During these last 1,260 days Jerusalem will be "tread under

101

foot" by the nations:

"...for it has been given to the nations: and they will tread under foot the holy city for 42 months (Three-and-a-half-years)."

(Revelation11:2)

These last three-and-a-half years will be in contrast to the first three-and-a-half years. The first period will seem to bring the peace that Israel fought and died for so long. The second period will be characterized by the Antichrist's claims to be God, persecutions of believers, and war over the land of Israel.

It's a challenge to think about in which three-an-a-half year period these two prophets will be needed most: the peaceful period when Antichrist helps defend and protect them with deception; or the last when all hell breaks loose on Israel.

There is no reason why we should limit trying to fit their ministry exactly within one of these two periods. I believe it's very likely these two will start their ministry sometime in the first "peaceful" three-and-a-half years, and finish sometime during the last three-and-a-half years.

Regardless of when they arrive on the scene, these two are destined to make big headlines. Israel's faithful God will use these two powerful preachers to proclaim God's plan. Some Bible scholars say these two witnesses will be Moses and Elijah. Tim LaHaye and Jerry B. Jenkins write in their book, *Are We Living in the End Times?* "Moses and Elijah are the two most influential men in the history of the Jews. Moses introduced God's written law to Israel and wrote the first five books of the Old Testament. Elijah was the first of the writing prophets and started the school of prophets. Moses and Elijah accompanied Jesus and the three disciples when He was 'transfigured before them' on the mount...The two witnesses are said to reproduce the very miracles that Moses and Elijah performed while on earth."[1]

Whoever they are, they will be instruments of judgment on Jerusalem's enemies. Look at the power they display. They are able to turn the waters into blood, smite the earth with plagues, cause it to stop raining, and call down other destructive things as judgment. It's easily observed that the description of these powers is identical to those judgments described throughout Revelation as occurring during the last seven-year period. God is going to use these two witnesses to bring some of these judgments upon those living at that time.

It's no wonder the world will rejoice when it hears the broadcast of their death. But what a surprise the world faces a few days later. Here's the amazing account:

"And when they have finished their testimony, the beast that

103

comes up out of the abyss will make war with them and overcome them and kill them. And their dead bodies will lie in the street of the great city which mystically is called Sodom and Egypt, where also their Lord was crucified. And those from the peoples and tribes and tongues and nations will look at their dead bodies for three-and-a-half days and will not permit their dead bodies to be laid in a tomb. And those who dwell on the earth will rejoice over them and make merry; and they will send gifts to one another, because these two prophets tormented those who dwell on the earth. And after the three-and-a-half days the breath of life from God came into them, and they stood on their feet; and great fear fell upon those who were beholding them. And they heard a loud voice from heaven saying to them, "Come up here". And they went up into heaven in the cloud, and their enemies beheld them."

(Revelation 11: 7-12)

There won't be any doubt about identifying this event! This is the first time in history that the world has the technology for this prophecy to be fulfilled. The world will foolishly rejoice over their deaths to the point of "party-time" gift exchange. The evening news will show their lifeless bodies for three-and-a-half days until the breath of life from God revives them. The party will end abruptly as fear and a great earthquake crashes the foolish party.

These two witnesses will no doubt have a major influence on Jewish minds questioning the divinity of the new world leader claiming to be their Messiah the Antichrist. And you can just imagine how furious this Antichrist will be as these two witnesses and the emerging presence of the 144,000 Jewish Witnesses challenge his kingship. I like what Dr. Jack Van Impe with Roger F. Campbell says in their book, *Israel's Final Holocaust,* "It is not difficult to imagine the reaction of the world dictator to these who publicly proclaim the end of his reign and announce the coming kingdom of Christ. His anger will explode in an avalanche of persecution. This dictator will announce a campaign to destroy the Jewish race once and for all. He will blame them for every ill on earth...The hatred and animosity of the Hamans and Hitlers of history will culminate in this end-time evil ruler."[2]

It's obvious to me that the ministry of the two witnesses will complement the ministry of the 144,000 Jews who will be sealed and anointed by God to proclaim the truth. While most of the world is receiving a mark on the hand or forehead to be able to operate economically, these 144,000 receive the seal of God on their forehead.

"...Do not harm the earth or the sea or the trees, until we have sealed the bondservants of our God on their foreheads. And I heard the number of those who were sealed, one hundred and forty-four thousand sealed from every tribe of the sons of Israel."

(Revelation 7:3, 4)

105

"Then I looked, and behold, the Lamb was standing on Mount Zion, and with Him one hundred and forty-four thousand, having His name and the name of His Father written on their foreheads."

(Revelation 14:1)

Chapter 13

World Leader Claims He's God

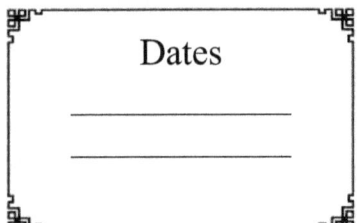

Dates

_____

_____

"...and the man of lawlessness is revealed, the son of destruction who opposes and exalts himself above every so-called god or object of worship, so that he takes his seat in the temple of God, displaying himself as being God." (2 Thessalonians 2:3, 4)

The history of Israel and the Jewish religion, Judaism, depended greatly on its use of a temple in Jerusalem. Priests conducted worship and offerings of animal sacrifices. And once a year, on the Day of Atonement, the High Priest entered into what was called the "most holy place" (Exodus 26:33) or "Holy of Holies" in the temple. He was the only one allowed to enter this area, since the presence of God was there to give forgiveness for sins.

Two such temples have been built over the last 3,000 years. The last one was destroyed in 70 AD when the Romans sacked Jerusalem. Since then, many nations have had control over the area and at present there is no temple.

Yet, prophecy tells us that a world leader that makes a peace treaty with Israel will break that treaty, go into the temple's "most holy place" and declare himself God. This is referred to by the prophet Daniel as the "Abomination of Desolation" since God abhors what this blasphemer will do.

> "And he will make a firm covenant with the many for one week, but in the middle of the week he will put a stop to sacrifice and grain offering: and on the wing of abominations will come one who makes desolate, even until a complete destruction, one that is decreed, is poured out on the one who makes desolate."
>
> (Daniel 9:27)

> "And forces from him will arise, desecrate the sanctuary fortress, and do away with the regular sacrifice. And they will set up the abomination of desolation." (Daniel 11:31)

> "And from the time that the regular sacrifice is abolished, and the abomination of desolation is set up, there will be 1,290 days."
>
> (Daniel 12:11)

"Therefore when you see the ABOMINATION OF DESOLATION which was spoken of through Daniel the prophet, standing in the holy place (let the reader understand), then let those who are in Judea flee to the mountains; let him who is on the housetop not go down to get the things out that are in his house; and let him who is in the field not turn back to get his cloak. But woe to those who are with child and to those who nurse babes in those days! But pray that your flight may not be in the winter, or on a Sabbath; for then there will be a great tribulation, such as has not occurred since the beginning of the world until now, nor ever shall. And unless those days had been cut short, no life would have been saved; but for the sake of the elect those days shall be cut short."

(Matthew 24:15-22)

These verses clearly point to a world leader who wants to be known as God, the Messiah, the Savior of mankind. He is referred to throughout the Bible as Antichrist, since he is a false Christ against (anti) everything Christ stands for.

Scholars speculate on other details of the Antichrist's entrance into the "Holy of Holies". Charles Dyer, associate professor of Bible exposition at Dallas Theological Seminary writes, "The abomination will be an image of the beast that will be set up in the temple in Jerusalem. (Revelation 13:14)."[1]

This event marks the midway point of a seven-year treaty. It will be a humiliating experience for the Jews who once believed in this impostor. And, as Matthew 24:15-22 reads, the Jews are told to "flee to the mountains" when they see this happening. Let's hope many will have the wisdom enough to follow this warning.

There is another shocking event that will involve this Antichrist that will bring awe and worship to him. Look what the Scriptures say:

"And I saw one of his heads as if it had been slain, and his fatal wound was healed. And the whole earth was amazed and followed after the beast." (Revelation 13:3)

There will be plenty of TV coverage on this one! The world community will be stunned and mesmerized by the miraculous recovery of their new world leader as he rebounds from some kind of deadly wound. Since our Lord is the only one who can give new life or resurrect anybody, I believe this wound is miraculously healed, but he himself does not rise from death to life again.

The beast in John's revelation has 10 horns and seven heads. One of these heads receives this fatal wound. Now since the meaning for the symbolism "heads," means a national leader or king, we shouldn't necessarily think that the wound is to his head. It is saying that he is the "head" and suffers a fatal-like wound.

We know that this leader is our infamous Antichrist because of

110

what is told to us later. As a leader of this ten-nation alliance, he receives worship from the world since they believe no one can wage war against him.

"...and they worshipped the dragon, because he gave his authority to the beast; and they worshipped the beast, saying, "Who is like the beast, and who is able to wage war with him?" And there was given to him a mouth speaking arrogant words and blasphemies; and authority to act for forty-two months was given to him. And he opened his mouth in blasphemies against God, to blaspheme His name and His tabernacle, that is, those who dwell in heaven. And it was given to him to make war with the saints and to overcome them; and authority over every tribe and people and tongue and nation was given to him. And all who dwell on the earth will worship him, everyone whose name has not been written from the foundation of the world in the book of life of the Lamb who has been slain. If anyone has an ear, let him hear."

(Revelation 13:4-9)

You should know that the dragon referred to is Satan himself. In this passage he gives his power to the beast, the ten- nation federation, through this wounded leader. In fact, it is taught that Satan is thrown out of heaven and possesses the Antichrist to give him amazing powers.

"How you have fallen from heaven, O star of the morning, son of

111

the dawn! You have been cut down to the earth, you who have weakened the nations! But you said in your heart, "I will ascend to heaven; I will raise my throne above the stars of God, and I will sit on the mount of assembly in the recesses of the north. I will ascend above the heights of the clouds; I will make myself like the Most High." Nevertheless, you will be thrust down to Sheol, to the recesses of the pit. Those who see you will glaze at you, they will ponder over you, saying, "Is this the man who made the earth tremble, who shook kingdoms, who made the world like a wilderness and overthrew its cities, who did not allow his prisoners to go home?" (Isaiah 14:12-17)

"And there was war in heaven, Michael and his angels waging war with the dragon. And the dragon and his angels waged war, and they were not strong enough, and there was no longer a place found for them in heaven. And the great dragon was thrown down, the serpent of old who is called the devil and Satan, who deceives the whole world; he was thrown down to the earth, and his angels were thrown down with him." (Revelation 12:7-9)

I realize this may be strong medicine for many to swallow. So many people still cringe over the possibility that there really exists a living personality called the devil. But there is a devil. And everyone that continues in their sinful ways is being tricked by him to reject Christ's free offer of forgiveness. He will also trick the world into

112

believing this leader is a powerful divine world savior, even though he wages a war of extermination on the saints and the Jews.

There's something you need to know about Satan that will help you realize his tactics. He wants to be like God, which means he wants to be worshipped. Satan-worshipping cults throughout the world demonstrate some of his success. During these last few years of the Tribulation, he builds an image and requires the world to worship it.

"And he deceives those who dwell on the earth because of the signs which it was given him to perform in the presence of the beast, telling those who dwell on the earth to make an image to the beast who had the wound of the sword and has come to life. And there was given to him to give breath to the image of the beast, that the image of the beast might even speak and cause as many as do not worship the image of the beast to be killed."

(Revelation 13:14-15)

As you can see, there are several places in the Bible where we are told how this "beast" will desire to devour the world, especially the Jews. And they have been given ample warning to "flee to the mountains".

One of the places the Jews will have to choose from is an historical site called Petra, inside Jordan. Dr. N.W. Hutchings, author

113

of "Petra in History & Prophecy", calls it "the most famous ghost town on earth," the one place that the Jews will flee to for a hiding place when the anger of the Antichrist breaks forth during the last half of the Tribulation, three-and-a-half years. Hutchings gives us a brief sketch of Petra: "Petra is located approximately one hundred eighty miles south of Amman and seventy-five miles north of Aqaba in Jordan. Its biblical names are Mount Seir and Sela. ...Petra is also described by the prophets as the rocky nest of the eagle, the city of Esau, and the stronghold of the Edomites."[2] It is the second most mentioned city in the Bible, Jerusalem being the first.

Tourists travel to this spectacular city of twenty square miles. Bedouins, who live in tents, help guide the tourists through rock formations that serve as the entrance to Petra – "one of the most fantastic rock formations on earth -- El Ciq."[3] The Ciq itself is 6000 feet long, 12 to 30 feet wide, with walls shooting up 300 to 500 feet high. The temperature climbs to over 100 degrees F, with no wind, and only a few inches of rain annually. Then once you've made this challenging entrance, you are shocked at the awesome display of a world of rock dwellings and temples, carved out of the sandstone cliffs. Hutchings says, "It would appear that there is a basis for the belief by some that Petra was formed by a combination of volcanic and earthquake activities."[4]

The city used to get its water from channels chiseled into the mountain walls that went back to a place called Ain Musa (the Springs of Moses), a place two miles away where spring water pours from rock formations, believed to be where Moses struck a rock to bring forth water.[5]

One of the photos shown in Hutchings' book shows just one view of a mountainside with hundreds of caves and dwellings carved into its landscape. He notes: "The thousands of caves could easily provide homes for a million people."[6] So, will caves for a million be enough for the fleeing Jews?

At least three places in the Bible talk about Israel being attacked badly, admonished to flee, being exiled, and losing major portions of its population. One of them was Matthew 24:16-21, quoted earlier in this chapter where it says they should flee to the mountains. The other two are in Zechariah, where in chapter 13:8 he says, "It will come about in all the land, declares the Lord, that two parts in it will be cut off and perish; but the third will be left in it." And chapter 14:2 says, "…the city (Jerusalem) will be captured, the houses plundered, the women ravished, and half of the city exiled, but the rest of the people will not be cut off from the city."

About 9 million live in Israel at present. But with large numbers being killed as mentioned above, perhaps only a million or less will represent the "remnant" expected to live and see Christ's visible return.

Hutchings also gives some strong "clues" as to why he believes Petra will be the hiding place. Here are several of them: 1)

Accessibility: Petra is 120 miles southwest of Jerusalem. It is nearby but would be very hard to get to in the winter; 2) Geographically: mountainous area;3) Politically: The location has to be a difficult place for Antichrist's forces to reach, since they will be in control of all the world at that time, except one place - Jordan. Daniel 11:41, says, "He (Antichrist) will also enter the Beautiful Land (Israel), and many countries will fall; but these will be rescued out of his hand: Edom, Moab, and the foremost of the sons of Ammon." These ancient references are easily identified as the boundaries of modern Jordan. Perhaps Jordan was able to negotiate a special "hands-off" policy when the seven-year treaty was made; 4) Availability: large enough to house them. I have already shown how the city could hold about 1 million, the remnant of Jews escaping; 5) Geologically: Petra has many caves and caverns that could be considered "rooms" (in some translations, "chambers"). Isaiah 26:20 says, "Come, my people, enter into your rooms and close your doors behind you; hide for a little while until the indignation runs its course."[7]

When one sees all the prophecies that spell out what God is going to do, it is almost unbelievable. But then when you begin to see it actually HAPPEN, it will send goose bumps up and down your spine, especially if you have been incredulous all along. So, get ready when you witness an exodus to Petra! It may not be too late for you to drop to your knees in repentance and turn to Christ as your Savior. It won't be long before He appears in the sky with the rest of His army of believers!

Chapter 14

Armageddon

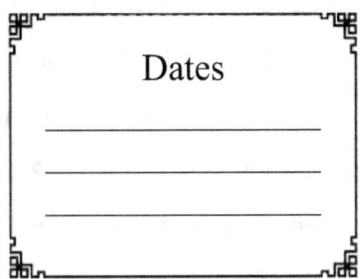

Dates

_____

_____

_____

"...And they gathered them together to the place which in Hebrew is called Harmagedon. And the seventh angel poured out his bowl upon the air; and a loud voice came out of the temple from the throne, saying, 'It is done'. And there were flashes of lighting and sounds and peals of thunder; and there was a great earthquake, such as there had not been since man came to be upon the earth, so great an earthquake was it, and so mighty." (Revelation 16:16-18)

Armageddon is a place in northern Israel in the plain of Jezreel. It is a hill or mound called *Megiddo* that was the scene of many ancient battles. And it will be the staging area for the armies of many nations as they plan to destroy Jerusalem.

"...for they are spirits of demons, performing signs, which go out to the kings of the whole world, to gather them together for the war of the great day of God, the Almighty."   (Revelation 16:14)

As you can see, no matter what the human explanation will be for so many nations marching towards Jerusalem (military, economic, religious, political, etc.), the real reason is found in the *spiritual* realm.

In this battle, the Lord is pouring out His final stages of judgment on Israel and those who oppose her. A great earthquake and 100-pound hailstones are just part of His intervention in this battle.

"And the great city (Jerusalem) was split into three parts, and the cities of the nations fell. And Babylon the great was remembered before God, to give her the cup of the wine of His fierce wrath. And every island fled away, and the mountains were not found. And huge hailstones about one hundred pounds each came down from heaven upon men; and men blasphemed God because of the plague of the hail, because its plague was extremely severe."

(Revelation 16:19-21)

Do you remember the events that precede this final war? One of these events, which I've called Israel at War with Russia, is still in recent memory. The Antichrist, as leader of the EU, has watched the supernatural defeat of the northern allied force that attacked Israel (Ezekiel 39:18-23). This was Russia and an Afro-Arab alliance. Those surviving this onslaught in Israel are burning the military debris as fuel, which will continue for seven years.

So, there is still a Jewish presence in Israel, although millions have gone. Many have been killed through persecution and many have fled to the mountains, Petra being the most likely destination. Yet despite all this, the 144,000 Jewish evangelists are spreading the gospel and nations are boiling angry because they can't be stopped. Even distant China sends an army marching towards Israel.

"And the sixth angel poured out his bowl upon the great river, the Euphrates; and its water was dried up, that the way might be prepared for the kings from the east."   (Revelation 16:12)

The Antichrist, leader of the EU, will move his forces into Israel to counter the troops coming from China in the east. And it appears that other national leaders (kings) will join sides and prepare to do battle over Israel (Revelation 16:14).

The question that must be nagging you is why are all these people so eager to converge on Israel to fight and die? What is so important or valuable to cause such turmoil?

As already noted, the real reason is spiritual. God's enemies,

Satan and his demons, are trying to destroy this precious holy city, Jerusalem. While God is obviously allowing this, He is using it as judgment on the Jews for their past rejection of His Son as well as their long history of breaking His laws.

On a more human level, we have to remember the on-going events during these last days. The effects of various nuclear exchanges, and the supernatural destruction that took place during the previous war (Russia's defeat in Israel)), have caused serious damage to the world. The book of Revelation describes how a third of the rivers, seas, and land are destroyed. Following these disasters, things still get worse. Read how the seven vials of judgment affect those remaining *before* this last main event – Armageddon:

"...a loathsome and malignant sore upon the men who had the mark of the beast and who worshiped his image."

(Revelation 16:2)

"...and every living thing in the sea died."   (Revelation 16:3)

"...and it (sun) was given to it to scorch men with fire."

(Revelation 16:8)

"And men were scorched with fierce heat; and they blasphemed the name of God who has the power over these plagues; and they

120

did not repent...”   (Revelation 16:9)

“...and his kingdom became darkened; and they gnawed their tongues because of pain.”   (Revelation 16:10)

Whatever the reasons are for these armies approaching Israel, you can be sure they are related to this horrible environment now affecting the world. Food and water will be the gold and silver of these closing months. And it's this desperate worldwide need for food that some scholars speculate brings the armies to Israel.

Did you know that the minerals deposited in the Dead Salt Sea in Israel have been estimated to be worth several trillion dollars? And one of the main minerals is potash, which is used for fertilizer and the manufacture of explosives. Do I need to say any more?

Any number of other reasons could explain why Israel would be under attack. And we can't overlook the spiritual battle going on here. We know that the false Christ (Antichrist) has tried to make the world worship and adore him as God. And there have been 144,000 Jewish preachers telling the world how the real Christ is yet to come. And believers have been executed for their resistance of Antichrist and his mark.

“And I heard the number of those who were sealed, one hundred and forty-four thousand sealed from every tribe of the sons of

121

Israel." (Revelation 7:4)

"After these things I looked, and behold, a great multitude, which no one could count, from every nation and all tribes and peoples and tongues, standing before the throne and before the Lamb, clothed in white robes, and palm branches were in their hands... And one of the elders answered, saying to me, 'These who are clothed in the white robes, who are they, and from where have they come?' And I said to him, 'My Lord, you know'. And he said to me, 'These are the ones who come out of the great tribulation, and they have washed their robes and made them white in the blood of the Lamb'". (Revelation 7:9, 13, 14)

Believers are being killed for their beliefs and strong outspoken rejection of the Antichrist's "new world order".

"And it was given to him to make war with the saints and to overcome them; and authority over every tribe and people and tongue and nation was given to him." (Revelation 13:7)

The Antichrist, as well as the rest of the world, are severely grieved. They will blame the world's disastrous condition on the fanaticism of the remaining faithful Christians (Jews and Gentiles) and attempt to end it once and for all. So the battle of Armageddon finally erupts.

Jesus returns with His army of resurrected saints to administer the final judgments, in preparation for starting a new 1,000-year reign (Millennium) with Himself as King:

"And the armies which are in heaven, clothed in fine linen, white and clean, were following Him on white horses. And from His mouth comes a sharp sword, so that with it He may smite the nations; and He will rule them with a rod of iron; and He treads the wine press of the fierce wrath of God, the Almighty. And on His robe and on His thigh, He has a name written, `KING OF KINGS, AND LORD OF LORDS'... And the beast (Antichrist) was seized, and with him the false prophet (apostate church leader) who performed the signs in his presence, by which he deceived those who had received the mark of the beast and those who worshiped his image; these two were thrown alive into the lake of fire which burns with brimstone." (Revelation 19:14-16, 20)

"Then the Lord will go forth and fight against those nations, as when He fights on a day of battle. And in that day His feet will stand on the Mount of Olives, which is in front of Jerusalem on the east; and the Mount of Olives will be split in its middle from east to west by a very large valley, so that half of the mountain will move toward the north and the other half toward the south."

(Zechariah 14: 3, 4)

By the way, if you wait until this phase of God's judgment to

123

repent, you've waited too long! Thus, the reason for the title of this book: *Armageddon, Are You Ready?* The Resurrection and Rapture have already occurred. Christ has already resurrected His saints. And most everyone in the world has already received the "mark of the beast", the personal number for their hand or forehead.

Observing the dates and fulfillment of prophecies leading up to this battle of Armageddon should get our serious attention before it's too late.

Chapter 15

The Second Coming of Jesus Christ

Date
_____

"For the Lord Himself will descend from heaven with a shout with the voice of the archangel, and with the trumpet of God; and the dead in Christ shall rise first. Then we who are alive and remain shall be caught up..."   (1 Thessalonians 4:16, 17)

"And the armies which are in heaven, clothed in fine linen, white and clean, were following Him on white horses."

(Revelation 19:14)

"...at the coming of our Lord Jesus with all His saints."

(1 Thessalonians 3:13)

T his is the glorious event all Christians wait and long for. It's the return of the Savior to bring His people the new resurrected life promised. And it will **happen in two distinct phases** (separated only by the pouring out of God's wrath) as indicated in these verses: 1 Thessalonians 4:16,17 - **Phase 1** is the Resurrection of all saints, including those believers alive at the time (called the "Rapture") when Christ suddenly removes His church on earth along with all who have died throughout the centuries as His followers; and Revelation 19:14 - **Phase 2** will consist of Christ and those same saints (resurrected in phase 1) returning to earth to fight in the battle of Armageddon and start a new millennium on earth.

The central figure of the Bible is Jesus Christ. In the Old Testament He is referred to as the coming Savior, Messiah, Redeemer, and offspring of Abraham who would be the King of the nation of Israel. In the New Testament, written after His first visit to earth (4 BC to 30 AD)[1], He is referred to as the Savior of all mankind, including not only Jews, but all those who will surrender to His will. Our dating system is divided around His birth. (BC, Before Christ; AD, Anno Domini which is Latin for "in the year of our Lord.")

After His teaching and preaching ministry had developed a strong following in Jerusalem, He was crucified by the religious and political leaders. He was a threat to their power, as He is always a

126

threat to any power contrary to His ways. His tragic death, miraculous resurrection, and ascension into the sky, were testimony to the divine nature of this Son of God and Son of Man.

He told His disciples about how He would return. They taught and wrote about His second coming, leaving us the written accounts of visions and prophecies that have warned generations what to watch for.

"And after He had said these things, He was lifted up while they were looking on, and a cloud received Him out of their sight. And as they were gazing intently into the sky while He was departing, behold, two men in white clothing stood beside them; and they also said, 'Men of Galilee, why do you stand looking into the sky? This Jesus, who has been taken up from you into heaven, will come in just the same way as you have watched Him go into heaven.'" (Acts 1:9-11)

"In My Father's house are many dwelling places; if it were not so, I would have told you; for I go to prepare a place for you. And if I go and prepare a place for you, I will come again, and receive you to Myself; that where I am, there you may be also." (John 14:2, 3)

IN BETWEEN Phase 1 and Phase 2

He will "come in just the same way..." as He did when the disciples watched Him ascend into the clouds. And when He returns

127

to resurrect and rapture believers (Phase 1), He will take us to "a place for you," for He says: "in My Father's house are many dwelling places." He has a purpose for these two phases: He is taking us to our new homes in heaven; the marriage supper of the Lamb, and the judgment seat of Christ. While the wrath of God is being poured out on the earth, the saints are being wed to our bridegroom, Jesus Christ, and judged for the kind of good works we did while following the Lord during our time on earth. Look how these two events fit into the future, in between the resurrection and rapture and return with His saints to the battle of Armageddon.

THE JUDGMENT SEAT OF CHRIST

"For we must all (believers) appear before the judgment seat of Christ, so that each one may be recompensed for his deeds in the body, according to what he has done, whether good or bad."

(2 Corinthians 5:10)

"For no man can lay a foundation other than the one which is Christ Jesus. Now if any man builds on the foundation with gold, silver, precious stones, wood, hay, straw, each man's work will be come evident; for the day will show it because it is to be revealed with fire, and the fire itself will test the quality of each man's work. If any man's work which he has built on it remains, he will receive a reward. If any man's work is burned up, he will suffer loss; but he himself will be saved, yet so as through fire."

(1 Corinthians 3: 11-15)

128

In these few verses, as well as others, the great difference is seen between the kind of judgment followers of Christ receive as opposed to everyone else. Because believers have made their peace with their God through Jesus and His plan of salvation, and their sins have been washed away, their only judgment is based on how well they served Him during the balance of their life. What type of "works" did they send up to show their faithfulness. These deeds are compared to materials ranging from gold to straw. What kind of dwelling will you have? Jesus has already laid the foundation (it cost Him His life, but it was a gift for us). But it will be your actions, your lifestyle, your ministry, your faithfulness that determines what type of dwelling you will have, whether it is a small shack or a grand mansion.

MARRIAGE OF THE LAMB

During this time in heaven as the world is suffering the wrath of God and the nations are fighting with every weapon they have, the Bridegroom will be joined to His bride, the bride of Christ.

"Let us rejoice and be glad and give the glory to Him, for the marriage of the Lamb has come and His bride has made herself ready. It was given to her to clothe herself in fine linen, bright and clean; for the fine linen is the righteous acts of the saints. Then he said to me, 'Write, Blessed are those who are invited to the marriage supper of

129

the Lamb.'"   (Revelation 19: 7-9)

Just a few verses later in Revelation 19, we are told that those clothed in fine linen are now descending towards earth with Him:

"And the armies which are in heaven, clothed in fine linen, white and clean, were following Him on white horses".   (Revelation 19:14)

This chapter focuses on the second and last phase of His coming – the return with His saints to earth. The first phase, when Christ suddenly resurrects all believers (the Resurrection and Rapture) to join Him in the sky, was focused on separately in chapter 8.

CHRIST'S RETURN TO EARTH

All the events unfolding during the Antichrist's reign, coupled with the judgments sweeping the nations during the seven-year period of Tribulation, set the stage for Christ's return. As a matter of fact, if He wouldn't intervene when He does, they would have destroyed themselves completely!

"And unless those days had been cut short, no life would have been saved; but for the sake of the elect those days shall be cut short."

(Matthew 24:22)

The world will be taking a beating. Man's hatred and zeal to rid the world of those he disagrees with, all in the name of "peace", leads us to the brink of destruction.

"Behold, He is coming with the clouds, and every eye will see Him, even those who pierced Him; and all the tribes of the earth will mourn over Him. Even so. Amen."　　　　　(Revelation 1:7)

The imposture of the real Messiah, the Antichrist, is slain in a moment, with only the appearance and breath of our Lord:

"And then the lawless one will be revealed whom the Lord will slay with the breath of His mouth and bring to an end by the appearance of His coming."　　　　　(2 Thessalonians 2:8)

He lands on the Mount of Olives and splits the earth from east to west.

"And in that day His feet will stand on the Mount of Olives, which is in front of Jerusalem on the east; and the Mount of Olives will be split in its middle from east to west by a very large valley, so that half of the mountain will move toward the north and the other half toward the south."　　　　　(Zechariah 14:4, 5)

A long, painful, horrible chapter of mankind will be over. But a new one begins for 1,000 years – the Millennium.

131

Chapter 16

The Millennium

"Blessed and holy is the one who has a part in the first resurrection; over these the second death has no power, but they will be priests of God and of Christ and will reign with Him for a thousand years."   (Revelation 20:6)

U
p until this time, the thousand-year reign by Christ, God has let man *do it his own way.* God has let man have all the kings and pharaohs and presidents and premiers he wanted to rule the nations. And man has totally failed to govern his world in a peaceful and just manner. In fact, we know the exact opposite has happened. Man has developed his mind and his sciences to great heights. But socially and spiritually man has failed miserably. Finally, God steps in just before we are ready to destroy ourselves completely (Second Coming of Christ) and sets up His rule for 1000 years, showing us how *it could have been* all these centuries.

The thousand-year reign of Christ, characterized by Bible scholars as the "Millennium", will begin the day Christ returns with

His church, in the clouds:

> "Behold, He is coming with the clouds, and every eye will see
> Him, even those who pierced Him; and all the tribes of the earth
> will mourn over Him. So it is to be.. Amen."   (Revelation 1:7)

> "...He may establish your hearts unblamable in holiness before
> our God and Father at the coming of our Lord Jesus with all His
> saints."   (1 Thessalonians 3:13)

What an absolutely thrilling time this will be! Not only does the
believer have the eternal promise of living with Christ forever, but
we also have this special period of reign on earth to look forward to.
It will be a demonstration to all the nations and religions that Christ
was the only true Son of God, the one prophet they should have
turned to earlier.

Let's consider what kind of a world Christ and His saints will be
facing when they return.

KINGDOM CONDITIONS

The world is in shambles. All of the destruction from the
judgments described in the book of Revelation has passed. A need
for reconstruction and healing is the only agenda on anyone's mind.

This is the moment in time that believers had hoped for down

133

through the centuries when they prayed, "Thy kingdom come; Thy will be done, on earth as it is in heaven." (Matthew 6:10) Christ's kingdom has come, and His will shall be done. This period will be similar to the way God originally intended for us to live when He put Adam and Eve in the Garden of Eden, before they sinned. Just look at some of the amazing changes this new period will experience.

"And the wolf will dwell with the lamb, and the leopard will lie down with the kid, and the calf and the young lion and fatling together; a little boy will lead them. Also, the cow and the bear will graze; their young will lie down together; and the lion will eat straw like the ox. And the nursing child will play by the hole of the cobra, and the weaned child will put his hand on the viper's den. They will not hurt or destroy in all My holy mountain, for the earth will be full of the knowledge of the Lord as the waters cover the sea."   (Isaiah 11:6-9)

"There is a real peace in this new world. Creation has been liberated from the curse of sin: "the creation itself also will be set free from its slavery to corruption…"   (Romans 8:21)

"And He will judge between many peoples and render decisions for mighty, distant nations. Then they will hammer their swords into plowshares and their spears into pruning hooks; nations will not lift up sword against nation, and never again will they train for war. And each of them will sit under his vine and under his fig tree, with no one to make them afraid, for the mouth of the Lord of hosts has spoken." (Micah 4:3, 4)

There will be no more wars! A reign of real peace will exist. Each will be able to feed himself as the earth yields its original abundance of fruits. The curse given in Genesis 3:17-19 will be lifted: "Cursed is the ground because of you (Adam); in toil you shall eat of it all the days of your life. Both thorns and thistles it shall grow for you..."

And look at the way our aging process changes:

"No longer will there be in it an infant who lives but a few days, or an old man who does not live out his days; for the youth will die at the age of one hundred and the one who does not reach the age of one hundred will be thought accursed." (Isaiah 65:20)

There will be long life, but death will still be with us. Those who somehow survived the judgments and the battle of Armageddon, will now populate and be governed by the Prince of Peace and all His saints. Death is not eliminated until *after* the thousand-year rule. "Death and Hades are thrown into the lake of fire" at that time (Revelation 20:14).

135

TYPES OF PEOPLE

Those enjoying the Millennium can be classified into two types.

The first type is comprised of all those described earlier as "saints or believers" who participated in the first Resurrection (Revelation 20:5). This is the Church, the Body of Christ, and Old Testament believers possessing a glorified body just like Christ. Remember how He could walk through walls after His resurrection (1 Corinthians 15:42-44; Luke 24:36, 37)? This group will have spiritual bodies and be able to perform on a higher level of knowledge and power than ever imagined. This extraordinary power will equip the saints to be co-rulers with Christ and be His "rod of iron" as He rules the nations during these 1000 years (Revelation 2:26, 27).

The second type of person living during this period are all those who survived the final days of the Tribulation, with all its horrible destruction. These are people who did not follow Christ when the great opportunity of the *Rapture occurred in the middle of the Tribulation,* but later saw the light at some stage during the last destructive years of judgment. They very likely heard the preaching of the 144,000 converted Jews, and became sincere, genuine believers who were never caught by the Antichrist and never accepted the mark of the beast. Among this group would also be small children who still did not have reasoning responsibility and whom the Lord considers innocent. This group of persons will not

136

have a glorified body, as the saints do, since they will not have experienced death. But they will benefit from the restoration of all living things as the curse on creation is lifted, and they begin a new age for mankind.

In case you're wondering what happened to all the others who might have survived the wrath of God when Christ returned with His saints, they are judged on the spot by Christ as described by Matthew:

> "But when the Son of Man comes in His Glory, and all the angels with Him, then He will sit on His glorious throne. And all the nations will be gathered before Him, and He will separate them from one another, as the shepherd separates the sheep from the goats; and He will put the sheep on His right, and the goats on the left. Then the King will say to those on His right, "Come, you who are blessed of My Father, inherit the kingdom prepared for you from the foundation of the world.... Then He will also say to those on His left, "Depart from Me, accursed ones, into the eternal fire which has been prepared for the devil and his angels."
>
> (Matthew 25:31-34, 41)

MILLENNIUM EVENTS

The last chapter of the prophet Zechariah's book gives an excellent picture of how Israel and Jerusalem fair in this new thousand-year period. A couple thousand years of roller-coaster experiences of obeying God, then rebelling against Him has finally culminated in victory. The promises to Abraham are fulfilled and a remnant of Jews can proclaim God's mercy and forgiveness forever.

"And the Lord will be king over all the earth; in that day the Lord will be the only one, and His name the only one...And people will live in it (Jerusalem), and there will be no more curse, for Jerusalem will dwell in security...Then it will come about that any who are left of all the nations that went against Jerusalem will go up from year to year to worship the King, the lord of hosts, and to celebrate the Feast of Tabernacles...And it will be that whichever of the families of the earth does not obey to go up to Jerusalem to worship the King, the Lord of Hosts-there will be no rain on them."   (Zechariah 14:9-17)

We see that the nations will be required to celebrate the Feast of Tabernacles, an autumn festival at the end of the fruit harvest when the people lived in shelters made of branches to give thanks for the harvest and remind themselves of how they had once lived in tents in the wilderness. The Jews celebrated two other festivals every year before the Feast of Tabernacles: the Passover and the Feast of Harvest (50 days after Passover, also called Pentecost).

These memorials will be held annually during the Millennium.

138

They will have an even greater significance as the curse on the ground has been lifted and greater harvests of crops are supplied by the Lord.

Look at another remarkable change that the Millennium brings:

"And he who overcomes, and he who keeps My deeds until the end, To him I will give authority over the nations; and he shall rule them with a rod of iron, as the vessels of the potter are broken to pieces, as I also have received authority from My Father."

(Revelation 2:26, 27)

It seems clear that despite all the blessings during this period, the surviving generations will continue to have their free will and a capacity to sin and disobey. They will not be robots, but will continue to have their original human nature, with its tendency to sin. The saints have been preserved to be co-rulers with Christ and will be His "rod of iron". One could speculate all day long what this might mean, but surely it is sufficient to say they will have authority to help administer Christ's righteous rule.

A lot of detail is not given in the prophecies about the Millennium, perhaps so we could dream for hours on how life will be and how God will treat this whole new generation. This is just another one of the many glorious surprises we all can look forward to experiencing when the time comes. And even though our curiosity will have to wait before it is satisfied, it's natural to want to ask,

139

"What about after the Millennium?"

In closing this chapter on the Millennium, we will take a quick glance at how God plans to deal with His creation after the Millennium. It will help give perspective to everything else that's happened, as well as create even more curiosity as we try to envision the "new earth and new heavens" He makes after this thousand-year period.

AFTER THE MILLENNIUM

A quick view of some of the events that take place after 1000 years:

"And when the thousand years are completed, Satan will be released from his prison, and will come out to deceive the nations which are in the four corners of the earth, Gog and Magog, to gather them together for the war; the number of them is like the sand of the seashore. And they came up on the broad plain of the earth and surrounded the camp of the saints and the beloved city, and fire came down from heaven and devoured them. And the devil who deceived them was thrown into the lake of fire and brimstone, where the beast and the false prophet are also; and they will be tormented day and night forever and ever."

(Revelation 20:7-10)

As you can see, even after the thousand years of righteous living, the world is still subject to deceit as Satan convinces the nations once again to try and destroy Jerusalem, the "beloved city". Most Bible scholars refer to this war as simply *God vs. Satan*. You can see who wins.

You wouldn't be normal if you didn't snap back and grumble, "But why would God do something like that? Why would He let Satan loose again, and allow another war?" I surely did.

Well, I'm reasonable and humble enough to say "I just don't know." But it just seems obvious that God is letting man come under a series of events that constantly test his faithfulness, just as He did with the nation of Israel. First, He shows His love and sets some laws. Then mankind is deceived and falls. Then God displays His mercy and patience to forgive those who repent and come back to Him. And then the cycle repeats itself. Yet we begin to see how God's grace and mercy are all that stand between us and damnation.

Now that the Millennium is over, and this final attempt by Satan is over, God has another huge surprise for us. One that perhaps we all have dreamed about since we could look up towards the heavens and wonder what it would be like to have a home in heaven.

"And I saw a new heaven and a new earth; for the first heaven and the first earth passed away, and there is no longer any sea. And I saw the holy city, new Jerusalem, coming down out of heaven from God, made ready as a bride adorned for her husband. And I heard a loud voice from the throne, saying "Behold, the tabernacle of God is among men, and He shall dwell among them, and they shall be His people, and God Himself shall be among them, and He shall wipe away every tear from their eyes; and there shall no longer be any mourning, or crying, or pain; the first things have passed away." And He who sits on the throne said, "Behold, I am making all things new." And He said, "Write, for these words are faithful and true." And He said to me, "It is done. I am the Alpha and Omega, the beginning and the end. I will give to the one who thirsts from the spring of the water of life without cost. *He who overcomes* shall inherit these things, and I will be his God and he will be My son. But for the cowardly and unbelieving and abominable and murderers and immoral persons and sorcerers and idolaters and all liars, their part will be in the lake that burns with fire and brimstone, which is the second death."

(Revelation 21:1-8)

I don't know about you, but these words, coming from the apostle John during his vision, are impressive and powerful. I can't see how anyone would doubt they are divinely inspired, with no human influence. They are in harmony with all other scripture and still reveal new plans for His creation.

A new earth and a new heaven will appear. Some scholars explain that this will be the same earth after its restoration. They argue that God restores all the old things, such as He restores the saints and made them new creatures. (1 Corinthians 5:17) Actually, I

142

wouldn't spend one moment debating whether it was restored or completely new. I'm just overjoyed that there will be such a place that God has planned for me.

A new Jerusalem comes down from heaven and hangs over the earth, a floating city where the saints abide. This also is a breathtaking new surprise that God has in store for us. The dimensions are given in Revelation 21:16 in old biblical units that indicate the city will either be triangular or cubical with the length, breadth, and height being 1400 miles each! What a city!

The great university administrator, professor, and author of "*The King is Coming*", Dr. H.L. Willmington, says of this city, "According to our present-day measurements, this city would be roughly 1400 miles long, high, and wide...Density studies of city populations assure us that every single one of 40 billion (the total number of people who have ever lived could easily be accommodated upon just the first 'foundational floor' of this marvelous 1400-layered metropolis."[1]

This passage also confirms other biblical references to the "second death". Those who rejected God's warnings and His mercy, "the unbelieving", will be cast into the lake of fire which is called the "second death." This "second death" is the one thing all of mankind should fear the most. The first death we all know about and understand. It's our physical death. The scriptures describe it as the separation of our spirit from our body. But the "second death" is the separation of our spirit from God, forever!

Look what it says in another reference in one of the last chapters of Revelation:

"And I saw a great white throne and Him who sat upon it, from whose presence earth and heaven fled away, and no place was found for them. And I saw the dead, the great and the small, standing before the throne, and books were opened; and another book was opened which is the book of life; and the dead were judged from the things which were written in the books, according to their deeds. And the sea gave up the dead which were in it, and death and Hades gave up the dead which were in them; and they were judged, every one of them according to their deeds. And death and Hades were thrown into the lake of fire. This is the second death, the lake of fire. And if anyone's name was not found written in the book of life, he was thrown into the lake of fire."

(Revelation 20:11-15)

The judgment of the unbelievers is not a pleasant subject. We all would rather avoid it. It is the final stage of the process God set up. All the spirits of those who have died not knowing the Son of God (John 3:18), are brought forth to be judged for the degree of their sin, and "thrown into the lake of fire".

Is there anyone up until now, that does not understand why all the preachers and evangelists keep proclaiming how *we must be saved*? Saved from what? Saved from this second death! Saved from hell for eternity! Saved from a spiritual separation from God forever!

> "For God so loved the world, that He gave His only begotten Son, that whoever believes in Him should not perish, but have eternal life. For God did not send the Son into the world to judge the world; but that the world should be saved through Him. He who believes in Him is not judged; he who does not believe has been judged already, because he has not believed in the name of the only begotten Son of God. He who believes in the Son has eternal life; but he who does not obey the Son shall not see life, but the wrath of God abides on him." (John 3:16-18, 36)

BACK TO TODAY

Remember how we started this journey? We proposed that being open-minded and objective to what these prophecies have to say would be the key to understanding what God had in store for us. I propose that you continue with that open-minded approach as you watch for these prophecies to explode before your very own eyes, and then record them in this book. If what the Bible prophecies is truly divine, THEY WILL HAPPEN. And not in secret either. But the uninformed will not recognize them as you will. With today's technology, you'll see everything take place on your TV.

So, whereas this closing chapter ends on an extremely serious and somber note (the second death), the whole grand purpose of prophesy is to shock or jolt our interest in God's plan to *save us.* And now you know what He wants to save you from.

The bottom line can best be summed up in the last verse in Revelation 20:15: "**And if anyone's name was not found written in the book of life, he was thrown into the lake of fire.**"

Our names must get written into that book of life. Throw everything else to the wind. But get your name in His book! And don't overlook the possibility that perhaps a loving and merciful God plans to use this book, in your hand, as a guiding light to that end. May it be a happy ending.

Chapter 17

Will You Be Ready

"Know this first of all, that in the last days mockers will come with their mocking, following after their own lusts, and saying, 'Where is the promise of His coming? For ever since the fathers fell asleep, all continues just as it was from the beginning of creation.' But the day of the Lord will come like a thief, in which the heavens will pass away with a roar and the elements will be destroyed with intense heat, and the earth and its works will be burned up. Since all these things are to be destroyed in this way, what sort of people ought you to be in holy conduct and godliness, looking for and hastening the coming of the day of God... Therefore, beloved, since you look for these things, be diligent to be found by Him in peace, spotless and blameless, and regard the patience of our Lord to be salvation..."

(2 Peter 3:3, 4, 10-15)

The signs of the times are grim. Coming events, as prophesied in the Bible, are full of doom. There's no way of trying to whitewash over this. It has been my main purpose to point these events out as a warning to be ready. It is not my intent to leave you in shock, worried or depressed over the horror and destruction the world faces. But just as the Lord Jesus Christ does not want "any to perish but for all to come to repentance" (2 Peter 3:9), I too want to see you face these coming events with your faith and hope anchored in God Almighty.

If you've taken the time to read this book, you've already shown a genuine interest in your own future. You care about how you'll face these issues. And you probably care deeply about how your family and people across the world will face them. This is the kind of open and serious attitude absolutely vital to being ready.

The weather forecast for future events shows a series of major storms building in the upper atmosphere. Since they are moving our way, it makes good sense to prepare ourselves to survive the coming fury.

The introduction of this book described three types of persons that would be reading this: 1) the faithful believer; 2) the doubter; and 3) the hard-hearted. You need to honestly identify which one of the three best describes you. It will help you immensely in getting spiritually ready for your future. Because you see, the real need is for you to be a faithful believer. When you are living and thinking as a disciple of Christ, you will have the promise of eternal life. You will also have the inner strength and conviction to say no to the "mark of the beast" when that time comes. Better yet, you will be ready for the Resurrection and Rapture when believers are all caught up in the air to meet the Savior and Lord and forever be with Him.

So, where you are right now is important. If you are a doubter or a hard-hearted unbeliever, you need to start the process towards becoming a faithful believer. If you are a faithful believer, you need to be strongly grounded so that none of these events will shake your faith.

Remember, this is an issue of the heart. For the sake of argument, if all this prophecy stuff is real and there really is a divine being behind it, then He is the same one behind the miraculous writings known as the Bible, where all the thousand-year-old prophecies have been preserved. And this same divine author also gives us the formula for being ready.

I think an excellent place to begin, is by going to the end. What I mean is this: look at the purpose God has in bringing all these judgments on mankind. Then learn whether or not we can satisfy His purpose *before* going through it, or at worst, *as* we're going through it.

The first thing to recognize is that the tribulation that the world, and yes, even believers (saints), are going through demonstrates His patience and long suffering. And we have learned how it will eventually give way to His anger and vengeance. Part of the vision in Revelation pictures the saints asking God how much longer before He avenges their deaths.

"...and they cried out with a loud voice, saying, 'How long, O Lord, holy and true, wilt Thou refrain from judging and avenging our blood on those who dwell on the earth?'"   (Revelation 6:10)

"...and they said to the mountains and to the rocks, 'Fall on us and hide us from the presence of Him who sits on the throne, and from the wrath of the Lamb; for the great day of their wrath has come; and who is able to stand?'"   (Revelation 6:16, 1)

The day of God's wrath is always a threatening possibility. And it's not limited to this catastrophic period at the end of this age. Each person will have to face God's judgment for his sins or be saved by Christ's forgiveness.

"He who believes in the Son has eternal life; but he who does not obey the Son shall not see life, but the wrath of God abides on him."   (John 3:36)

So, whether we're facing our own consequences of sin personally, or we're facing the many tribulations in life, God's *wrath* is what we need to escape from.

The second vital thing we need to know is that God makes a way for us to escape, if we'll only wise up and take it. It's called *repentance*. It's an old-fashioned word, whose meaning has remained constant down through the ages. It was Jesus' main theme, and God's main objective for all the final judgments poured out during the Tribulation.

"...and saying, 'The time is fulfilled, and the kingdom of God is at hand; repent and believe in the gospel.'" (Mark 1:15)

"...and He said to them, 'Thus it is written, that the Christ should suffer and rise again from the dead the third day; and that repentance for forgiveness of sins should be proclaimed in His name to all the nations, beginning from Jerusalem.'" (Luke 24:46, 47)

"The Lord is not slow about His promise, as some count slowness, but is patient toward you, not wishing for any to perish but for all to come to repentance." (2 Peter 3:9)

"For the sorrow that is according to the will of God produces a repentance without regret, leading to salvation; but the sorrow of the world produces death." (2 Corinthians 7:10)

"And the rest of mankind, who were not killed by these plagues, did not repent of the works of their hands, so as not to worship demons, and the idols of gold and of silver and of brass and of stone and of wood, which can neither see nor hear nor walk; and they did not repent of their murders nor of their sorceries nor of their immorality nor of their thefts." (Revelation 9:20, 21)

"And men were scorched with fierce heat; and they blasphemed the name of God who has the power over these plagues; and they did not repent, so as to give Him glory... and they blasphemed the God of heaven because of their pains and their sores; and they did not repent of their deeds." (Revelation 16:9, 11)

Do you get the idea? Our creator wants us to be sorry for our sins, believe in His Son's sacrifice on the cross, receive Jesus as our Savior and Lord. Then He begins the process to help us make the changes in our behavior that prove our sincere repentance. Doing it His way, instead of "my way", will prepare us to face our own death or these judgments on earth, whichever comes first.

To summarize these principles in a step-by-step approach, consider these steps to getting ready to be saved from the penalties of sin, *death and judgment*, and be assured of eternal life.

Step 1: ACCEPT CHALLENGE

Determine your present state or condition. Be honest with yourself and admit your degree of doubt or hard-heartedness. Give God the benefit of the doubt so He may prove Himself to you. Purpose to seek Him.

"Here is a promise you can put your confidence in: 'And you will seek Me and find Me, when you search for Me with all your heart.'"

(Jeremiah 29:13)

Step 2: EXAMINE THE EVIDENCE

Check out the references noted in these pages to confirm the validity of the prophecies. The Bible speaks for itself. And watch continually to see the prophecies fulfilled right before your eyes on the world stage, on the TV, and in the newspaper.

Step 3: KNOW GOD'S PURPOSE

Our Lord's whole purpose for creating mankind was to love and fellowship with Him. He wants our praise, our gratitude, our attention, our loyalty, our prayers, our time, our service and our lives. In exchange for these, He gives us His unconditional love that will meet every human need for a happy and fulfilled life. He loves us so much that He planned a way for us to escape His own wrath by way of sacrificing His own son, Jesus. "For God so loved the world, that He gave His only begotten Son, that whoever believes in Him should not perish, but have eternal life." (John 3:16)

Step 4: RECOGNIZE THAT SIN SEPARATES

We need to admit the obvious. Our human nature has continually led us to act in ways we know are not right. Our thoughts and actions of

153

pride, jealousy, greed, hate, and lust have separated us from our holy God. Our consciences have been so seared, there is hardly a trace of any remembrance of what is good or evil anymore. And God cannot look upon or relate to this sin. He says, "...for all have sinned and fall short of the glory of God" (Romans 3:23). And "For the wages of sin is death, but the free gift of God is eternal life in Christ Jesus our Lord." (Romans 6:23)

Confession and agreement to this, our state of separation, is vital to the process of repentance. Absolutely vital! Without this conviction of sin, you will feel no need for a Savior. So let the Spirit of God convict you of this truth.

"And He, when He comes, will convict the world concerning sin and righteousness, and judgment; concerning sin, because they do not believe in Me..."   (John 16:8, 9)

Step 5: KNOW ABOUT THE SACRIFICE

God bridged the separation caused by sin with a sacrifice. He purchased our right to come into a holy relationship with Him again because the penalty for our sins was paid for by His only son, Jesus Christ. This gift of love is the only solution to our sin problem of separation.

"Now I make known to you, brethren, the gospel which I preached to you, which also you received, in which also you stand, by which also you are saved, if you hold fast the word which I preached to you, unless you believed in vain. For I delivered to you as of first importance what I also received, that Christ died for our sins according to the Scriptures, and that He was buried, and that He was raised on the third day according to the Scriptures, and that He appeared to Cephas, then to the twelve."   (1 Corinthians 15:1-5)

"Jesus said to him, "I am the way, and the truth, and the life; no one comes to the Father, but through Me."   (John 14:6)

That's why it's so important for missionaries to go out into all parts of the world. They carry this life-saving message. They realize how important it is for the world to hear and know this fact.

But knowing it is not the end of the process. Be very careful not to stop here, with only an intellectual knowledge. You must take the next step which is your personal response to God's offer.

Step 6: BELIEVE AND RECEIVE

It is not enough to have a head knowledge of God's love and sacrifice by way of His Son's death and resurrection. Yes, the hearing and knowing of God's word is vital. *But it must now go from a head knowledge to a heart conviction.* The last step in this process of repentance leading to salvation is receiving Christ into your heart and letting Him be your Savior and Lord.

155

"Behold, I stand at the door and knock; if anyone hears My voice and opens the door, I will come into him, and will dine with him, and he with Me."   (Revelation 3:20)

"But as many as received Him, to them He gave the right to become children of God, even to those who believe in His name."

(John 1:12)

"And the witness is this, that God has given us eternal life, and this life is in His Son. He who has the Son has the life; he who does not have the Son of God does not have the life. These things I have written to you who believe in the name of the Son of God, in order that you may know that you have eternal life."   (1 John 5:11-13)

This is where you may find a struggle. Because this is where the *will* is involved. You must humble yourself to let God's laws govern your life. We're used to doing things *our way*. This last step is like a line in the sand. When you cross over it, you inherit a treasury of blessings that sound too good to be true. You are actually "born again" according to scripture (John 3:3). And the world will tell you that you don't deserve these blessings and can't really be sure of them. But as a new believer, you will somehow know they belong to you. The Spirit of God will give you this inward witness.

Step 7: ENJOY THE BENEFITS

This my friend is what it's all about. Being ready is much more than protection from catastrophe, judgment, and death. It is claiming your divine birth rights to what God originally intended for you from the very beginning - before sin got in the way.

Once you are born again, your spirit is regenerated by the Spirit of God. You and He become One, united and related for the first time. You pass from death unto life, from darkness to light. You inherit the right to be called a son of God. And you have been adopted and received into the family of God.

God gives you His Spirit to dwell in you and assure you that you belong to Him. Your name is written in the Book of Life. (Some scriptures indicate that your name is written in the Book of Life at birth, even conception, but can be erased at the end of your life if you rejected Christ). Your salvation and eternal life are secured, not because of your good works, but because of His sacrifice (Ephesians 2:8, 9).

You now have the power and new desire within you to live a life of faith and conquer all the habitual sins you were used to committing. These will begin to fall away like dried up fruit from an old tree. And they will be replaced with new fruit called the "fruit of the Spirit". These are the real rewards everyone is seeking

157

for. "The fruit of the Spirit is love, joy, peace, patience, kindness, goodness, faithfulness, gentleness, self-control..." (Galatians 5:22)

Many other benefits are promised to the faithful believer. And we have a lifetime to experience them. Don't let any obstacle stand in your way of taking these seven steps towards your God. Be courageous. You can't afford to be without the Lord's Spirit and army of angelic helpers available to you. Be ready to face your future – not alone in fear or uncertainty, but in confidence and faith in God's merciful plan of salvation.

EPILOGUE

It hit me as I researched the mission of the two miracle workers and the 144,000 Jewish witnesses who appear during the last seven years of judgment. The world will have an abundance of proof and testimony pointing to the real Messiah and how to repent and follow Christ, knowing full well it will cost them their lives as many of them will become martyrs.

I thought, will they really need my book to contribute towards their decision of a lifetime? With all the miracles, disasters, judgments, death, sufferings, earthquakes, wars, persecutions, rumors, lies, and spiritual deception that will abound in these days, will they need a calm, objective, honest warning written years back to help put it all in perspective? Could the biblical facts clearly stated, categorized, and even dated (by themselves) make a difference? The answer I heard in my spirit was a long and quiet peace that grew to an amazing, energetic "YES".

So, as one last thought, I want to recommend a few simple practical things you can do to be ready for the fulfillment of these prophecies.

First, be sure to keep this book on your shelf in a place you can refer back to it as the prophecies develop. Write down the dates in the spaces provided in the beginning of each chapter. This will *prove to you* and your family that these prophecies, and the entire Bible, are inspired by the Lord and that your spiritual readiness is more and more paramount.

Second, use the convenient Summary of Events (at the back of the book) as a reminder. It lists the coming events with a space for you to record the date. This will help you to be mindful of world events as they unfold.

Third, be sure that you take seriously the seven steps to being ready talked about in the last chapter. No matter what your present condition or attitude is now, if you will give yourself a chance to be open and honest with God, you'll be surprised at how willing He is to respond to you. There are countless stories of how defiant and hard-hearted souls have cried out to God in one last desperate attempt to find meaning to life and found their answer. God met them in their moment of honest desperate truth when they admitted their need and His ability to meet it. I don't suggest you wait for a desperate moment. But if you do, remember the promise in Jeremiah 29:13: "And you will seek Me and find Me when you search for Me with *all your heart*." This is a promise you can count on.

And lastly, I want to encourage you not to be a lone ranger. Don't try to go your own spiritual way. The Lord intended for us all to be an integral member of a family, serving and helping each other. He called this family His church. It's not a building or a place, but the body of believers. And unfortunately, it has suffered some serious blows down through history to the present age.

Many of the criticisms leveled against the church are justified. It has not been the perfect expression of Christ's character that it claims to be. It has failed in many ways. Its hypocrisy has been its greatest sin, for how can a needy world respect the church's message of living a godly life when it turns around and falls into sin time and time again.

But in its defense, I would point out that the church was never meant to be perfect. It is in fact a hospital for sinners, where we are to congregate to get spiritual help. Obviously, there is a process involved in learning to follow Christ. And many of us trip and stumble along the way. The world calls this hypocrisy, while Christ calls it *sanctification* – a process of getting all areas of our life under His divine control.

So, while the church has been the brunt of a lot of criticism, we are still taught that it is the physical representation of Christ, the Body of Christ, which we are commanded to join in order to obey the Word of God and contribute our spiritual gifts.

The bottom line is that anyone who wants to please God, love His fellow man, and grow spiritually, needs to be a part of a local church. Don't be fooled into thinking that watching the TV evangelist is enough. It doesn't even come close. Find yourself a church that preaches and lives the truth taught in the Bible. Let their community reputation, your good common sense, and the inner witness of the Spirit of God tell you which one to join. Then join.

161

Summary of Events

Leading to Christ's Visible Second Coming

The whole purpose of this book has been to boil biblical prophecy down to a list of critical events we should be watching for. They are not necessarily listed in the exact order in which they will occur but in the same order as the chapters where they were mentioned. Again, it will be *you the reader who will prove God right and prove His Bible 100% accurate. It will be you who set the dates as they unfold before your very eyes. And it will be you who decides whether you will believe the propaganda of the world and their new leader, or the truth as you build it with the blocks of fulfilled prophecies laid each time you set the date on these pages.*

Chapter 1   Signs of the End Times

- Watch for continued increase of famines and earthquakes
  .... (No dates necessary)

- Watch for many new religious fanatics and cults
  .... (No dates necessary)

- Watch for the breakdown of society as mankind breaks God's laws ……... (No dates necessary)

- Watch for even more wars and threats of wars

    ………… (No dates necessary)

- Watch for Jews to migrate from all around the world to Israel

    ………….... (No dates necessary)

Chapter 2 Amazing Prophecies Already Fulfilled

- Dates for these prophecies are already recorded in this chapter

    …………….(No dates necessary)

Chapter 3 Seven Years of Trouble

- A major seven-year peace treaty, brokered by the EU leader (the Antichrist), will be signed by many nations. This will also be the beginning of troubles for the Jews as the last seven years of judgment God promised to them begins

    _____(date)

Chapter 4 Europe Takes Charge

- New EU leader gains notoriety as a charismatic politician (Antichrist) and strengthens the European Union with new economy, military, and political power.

    _____(date)

Chapter 5 Antichrist Brokers Israel's Peace

- EU leader (Antichrist) brokers a seven year Peace Treaty

163

..............(Same as Chapter 3)

Chapter 6   Israel at War with Russia

- A Russian-Arabian-African alliance invades Israel and is defeated supernaturally by God. It will take seven months to bury the dead and seven years to burn the weapons.

_____(date)

Chapter 7   Jerusalem's Temple is Reconstructed

- Peace Treaty allows the Jews to rebuild and use their Temple.

_____ (date)

- Midway through Peace Treaty, the EU leader (Antichrist) claims to be God, enters the Temple, and demands that the Jews, and the world, worship him.

_____(date)

Chapter 8   The Resurrection and Rapture

- Believers (Christians) around the world will be snatched up to heaven as Christ returns visibly and removes them before God's wrath begins. Chaos erupts because of the missing.

_____(date)

Chapter 9   Mark of The Beast

- A new economic system is imposed on the world as the Antichrist calls for a mark to be placed on the right hand or forehead of everyone in order to buy or sell.

_____(date)

Chapter 10 Alliance Made in Hell

- A charismatic religious leader will rise to world stature and unite with the Antichrist to control world events and require everyone to worship an image he places in the Temple.

_____ (date)

Chapter 11 Sin Topples the Church

- Churches & religions will join together abandoning biblical truth for the sake of unity and selling out (prostituting) its faith. True believers will be persecuted and the Apostate church is born.

_____(date)

Chapter 12 Two Powerful Miracle Makers

- Two Jewish prophets will proclaim God's message of repentance and perform Old Testament type miracles for three-and-one-half years.

_____(date)

- The two witnesses are killed and left to rot in the streets of Jerusalem as they are viewed on TV for three-and-a-half days of holiday celebration.

_____(date)

- God revives the two witnesses before the eyes of the world as they rise to Heaven in a cloud.

  _____(date)

- 144,000 Jews are sealed (marked & protected) by God to preach repentance and complete the Great Commission of preaching the gospel to whole world.

  _____(date)

Chapter 13 World Leader Claims He's God

- Midway through Peace Treaty, the EU leader (Antichrist) claims to be God, enters the Temple, and demands that the Jews, and the world, worship him...(Same as Chapter 7)

- Antichrist begins a long campaign of persecution against the Jews who flee to the mountains to safe areas such as the rock city of Petra in Jordan.

  _____(date)

Chapter 14 Armageddon

- Nations send forces to the plain of Jezreel where the mountain called Megiddo in Israel is located. They are there to destroy Israel.

  _____(date)

- An army from the Orient comes from the east to join in the destruction of Israel

_____(date)

- The Antichrist's world empire is destroyed with the appearance of Christ and His Saints when the Second Coming occurs at the Mount of Olives in Jerusalem......

_____(date)

Chapter 15 The Second Coming of Jesus Christ

- The visible return to earth of Jesus Christ with His Saints to stop the destruction of Jerusalem and to begin His thousand-year reign on earth (Millennium). (Same as Chapter 14)

ENDNOTES

Chapter 2

[1] Josh McDowell, *Evidence That Demands a Verdict*
(San Bernardino, Ca.: Campus Crusade for Christ, 1972), p. 175

[2] Ibid, pp. 180-181

Chapter 3

[1] Josh McDowell, *Evidence That Demands a Verdict*
(San Bernardino, Ca.: Campus Crusade for Christ, 1972), p. 179

[2] Ibid, p. 181

[3] Charles H. Dyer, *The Rise of Babylon: Sign of the End Times*
(Wheaton, Illinois: Tyndale House Publishers, Inc., 1991), p. 187

Chapter 4

[1] C.S. Lovett, *Latest Word on the Last Days* (Baldwin Park, Ca.:
Personal Christianity Chapel, 1980), pp. 82-83

[2] Dr. David Jeremiah, *Escape The Coming Night* (Nashville, Tn: W
Publishing Group, 1990), p.179

[3] Charles H. Dyer, *The Rise of Babylon: Sign of the End Times*
(Wheaton, Illinois: Tyndale House Publishers, Inc., 1991), p. 124

Chapter 6

[1] Hal Lindsey, *The Late Great Planet Earth* (Grand Rapids; Zondervan; 1970) p. 65

[2] Ibid, p. 65

[3] Ibid, p. 64-65

[4] Ibid, p. 68

[5] Ibid, p. 69

[6] Ibid, p. 70

[7] Ibid, p. 70

[8] Ibid, p. 70

Chapter 7

[1] David Alexander, Patricia Alexander, *Eerdmans' Handbook to the Bible* (Grand Rapids, Mi.: William B. Eerdmans Publishing Company, 1973), p. 254

[2] H.L. Willmington, *The King is Coming* (Wheaton, IL: Tyndale House Publishers, Inc.,1991), pp.130-131

[3] Ibid, p. 133

[4] The Temple Institute Web page (www.templeinstitute) 2/1/2002

[5] Ibid

[6] Ibid

[7] Wilmington, op.cit, p.135

[8] David Reagan, *The Middle East Crisis In Biblical Perspective* (McKinney, TX: Lamb & Lion Ministries, 2000), **Tape**

[9] Wilmington, op.cit, p.139

[10] Hal Lindsey, *There's A New World Coming* (Eugene, OR: Harvest House Publishers, 1973), pp.148-149

[11] Ibid, p. 141

[12] The Temple Institute Web Page

Chapter 8

[1] John Shorey, *The Window of the Lord's Return* (www.Tribulationtruth.com, August, 2010) p.92

Chapter 9

[1] David Streitfeld, *A Chip ID That's Only Skin-Deep*, Los Angeles Times, Dec. 19, 2001

Chapter 11

[1] C.S. Lovett, *Latest Word on the Last Days* (Baldwin Park, Ca.: Personal Christianity Chapel, 1980), pp. 103-105

[2] Ibid, p.93

[3] Ibid, p.94-95

Chapter 12

[1] Tim LaHaye & Jerry B. Jenkins, *Are we Living in The End Times* (Tyndale House Publishers, Inc., 1999), pp.292-293

[2] Dr. Jack Van Impe with Roger F. Campbell, *Israel's Final Holocaust* (Jack Van Impe Ministries, 1979). pp. 145, 147

Chapter 13

[1] Charles H. Dyer, *The Rise of Babylon: Sign of the End Times* (Wheaton, Illinois: Tyndale House Publishers, Inc., 1991), p. 189

[2] N. W. Hutchings, *Petra In History & Prophecy* (Oklahoma City, OK. Hearthstone Publishing Ltd, 1991), p.5

[3] Ibid, p.7

[4] Ibid, p.13

[5] Ibid, p.7

[6] Ibid, p.83

[7] Ibid, pp.142-147

Chapter 15

[1] Pat Alexander and David Alexander, *Eerdmans' Handbook to the Bible* (Grand Rapids, Michigan: William B. Eerdmans Publishing Company, 1973), p. 476

Chapter 17

[1] Wilmington, op.cit, p.199

www.ingramcontent.com/pod-product-compliance
Lightning Source LLC
Chambersburg PA
CBHW060941180626
46817CB00004B/1653